MYSTIC AGENT

A NOVEL BY
SIR PATRICK BIJOU

ABOUT THE AUTHOR

Sir Patrick Bijou is known for his role in the United Nations as a UN Ambassador for World Peace and a Senior Redemption Judge for the International Court of Justice and International Criminal Courts. He is also a Fund Manager and dynamic investment banker.

Sir Patrick is an eclectic writer who lives in the United Kingdom and was born in Georgetown and raised in London, England.

His authorship has earned him fame because his publications are not limited to a genre or theme, from adventurous, thrilling, romantic, criminal, and dramatic theme fictional novels. However, his experiences have influenced his diverse writing prowess.

He pursued several courses of study at several universities and declared two majors during his schooling, including Business and Economics. Finally, he obtained his doctorate in Economics and International banking.

In all these academic studies, though, the true treasures he took away are not the certificates (though those are very important), but instead, the experiences he had, the people he met, the foods he ate and even the places he stayed.

"In truth, I am a citizen of the world, and this greatly influences my writing., says Sir Patrick.

So, if you are already a fan of mine, I appreciate you. If you are not yet one, then what are you waiting for? Read a book and then read some more. I create characters that resonate with you and infuse life into all I write".

Finding my Books

Sir Patrick has written over 21 published fictional and non-fictional books across several genres and realises the need to make it easier for his readers to find his books.

www.sirpatrickbijou.com

I would appreciate if you would be kind enough to leave a review of this book.

Thank you for reading. I hope you have enjoyed it.

BOOK DESCRIPTION

A species on the verge of extinction, a childhood tragedy turned life-long obsession, and a series of mysterious kidnappings — these three things are interconnected. Captain Rhys Forester and Agent Analise Shepherd are about to find out how.

Rhys and his ilk are facing the consequences of a centuries-old disease — not enough female werewolves are being born and packs throughout are faced with the threat of extinction.

This drives the council to encourage werewolves to mate with humans. If it were up to Rhys, as an alpha, he wouldn't dream of it. Yet, it was necessary. As long as there was consent from human females, Weres were allowed their pick.

But when kidnappings started happening, Rhys and his pack were in danger of being discovered, especially since the one leading the charge is a highly intelligent, no-nonsense FBI agent like Analise Shepherd.

Working as the Riverton Police Captain, Rhys would rather rip her throat off and claw her eyes out before he would let a human take charge.

But even he can't deny that her fervor and focus were unparalleled. She was determined to figure the case out and find the missing girls if it's the last thing she does.

What Rhys doesn't know is that Analise has somewhat of a traumatic past. One that puts her on the path toward seeking justice, not just for her and her family but also for all of the victims in all of her cases.

However, there seems to only be room for one real alpha in this dynamic. As the two continually butt heads, they soon realized that they're more alike than they would even dare to admit.

Will Rhys and Analise be able to set aside their big egos long enough to actually work together and solve the case?

Will they realize that their hatred for each other is actually highly palpable and intoxicating sexual tension?

If yes, will this spell more trouble on the horizon?

Find out in "Mystic Agent" — an enthralling four-part werewolf romance series that is guaranteed to keep you glued to every page!

If you're looking for a spell-binding action thriller romance, then this series will be your next favorite book!

Scroll up, Click on "Buy Now with 1-Click", and Grab a Copy Today!

TABLE OF CONTENTS

CHAPTER 1

Rhys slammed the door to the Chevy pick-up in absolute fury. The force was so great he almost took the creaky old door right off its hinges.

"What crawled up his ass?" Micah asked Jameson to his left. Both were about as low of Omegas as was physically possible.

"I overheard Isa mention to one of the girls that there was a Council Meeting," he whispered back in a conspiratorial tone. "Must not a gone too good."

Micah's instant confusion morphed into concern. If Rhys was upset about the Council, then it was probably more serious than Micah had originally considered.

For his part, Rhys was far too absorbed in his own fury to give any attention to who or what might be in his way. Every door in his path was thrown shut with remarkable force in his wake. The only one who stood a chance of stopping this tirade was Isa but she wasn't so stupid as to approach the enraged barbarian of a male at this moment. Instead, the elderly woman waited with a sage-like patience for all the commotion to come to a deathly silence before she approached Rhys's quarters with a gentle rap at the door.

There was no answer.

Had she been anyone else, Isa would have taken that silence as answer enough. Instead, the woman gently pushed open the door to observe the man seated on the edge of his bed with his head buried hopelessly in his hands.

"There will be questions," she told him patiently. She knew better than to waste sweet lies on a man like Rhys.

"And how shall I answer them?" He answered more rhetorically than anything else. Rhys let out a defeated sigh and turned his cobalt blue eyes up to the old woman. "It was worse than you thought," he admitted. "The other packs are practically frothing at the mouth for it."

"Did you do as I asked?" She replied in the sing song tone that only age can afford. "We are small and insignificant in their eyes. Surely a delay for us is no threat to them."

"I did as you asked," he replied, albeit a bit more bitterly than he had wanted to convey. "But I'm pretty sure they all took it as a sign of weakness. I'm going to have the Wylders' hunting packs testing our territory by the end of the week." He looked up at her again, this time with frustration in his eyes. "And I don't think they even gave a damn about the time frames to begin with. Just stirred up a whole lotta trouble for nothing," he added, the bitterness back again.

If Isa was intimidated or guilt stricken, she certainly didn't show it. "It is done," she replied simply. "The pack needs to be informed."

Rhys sunk a little at this. There was just so much pressure. Everything was always on the verge of falling apart and he was always the bearer of bad news. He was pretty certain he knew how the pack would take the news he was about to deliver, too. The omega males would be tickled pink and everyone else would want his head on a stick. But what could he do about it? The decree didn't even come from the New World; It was straight from Bavaria itself.

With a heavy sigh, any lingering emotion was washed off of his face and Rhys rose, pushing past Isa without another word. To an outsider, he looked like a linebacker on his way to war. He always wore that face and demeanor. In fact, his stature was the only thing that kept the neighboring packs in check. No one wanted to mess with a 6'4 270 lb. alpha regardless of their numbers. Wearing the pissed off face all the time only added to the image.

As to be expected, the hallways of the complex were already partially cleared from Rhys's rather dramatic entrance. Bewildered Omegas pushed themselves hurriedly out of his way as he almost marched into the great room. The majority of the pack was already there, a hush of whispers coming to silence the moment Rhys cleared the hallway.

"You've all heard rumors, I'm sure, so it's probably better we get this all cleared up now," he announced, getting straight to business. "Many of you are suffering from the loss of your mate. Others have pointed out that we aren't producing enough female pups. Last year, of the twelve pups we sired, none were female."

There was a hush over the pack that spoke volumes. Everyone already knew this information as well as what was to come next.

"There's a disease. Near as they figure, any females who haven't already died from it probably won't, but... they said it's genetic. A lotta women won't be able to have pups and those who can?" He let his voice trail off as he maintained his stoic and distant demeanor. Inside, Rhys was howling for mercy. He swallowed hard as his eyes scanned his now captive audience. There was relief to be had in a lot of the younger women who undoubtedly wondered if the disease would strike them next, but there was also tremendous pain. Among the younger males, there was mostly just panic.

Rhys anticipated every one of these responses, but that anticipation did not make stomaching it any easier.

"The council's made a ruling," he announced, perhaps a little more harshly than he had intended to. "Females can take as many mates as they want; as many as it takes to produce a female pup. Council also wants us to..." Rhys swallowed again. This was the part he was actually dreading. "We are encouraged to mate with human stock," he finished in a gravelly tone.

The response was exactly what he had predicted. The Omegas had found nirvana. Everyone else was outraged. Rhys silently begged one of the omegas to make some sort of insensitive "Yesssssss" comments so he would have a legitimate excuse to rip someone in half, but no such comment came. In a way, it brought him a little pride to have his satisfaction delayed.

"The Forester pack isn't really rich," he started, coaxing his tone to sound inspirational. The truth was, he must have rehearsed this speech a dozen times. Isa had seen this decision looming in the future for years. "We don't have the best domain, we don't have the best resources, hell, our den is an abandoned coal mine. We've tasted desperate worse than most packs, I'd guess. And you know what? We keep our heads high even through the worst of it." He paused then to allow the compliment to take effect. He got about half of them, and none of them female. It was a start, but it wasn't as good as he was hoping for. "This isn't gonna be any different. We aren't gonna do this like a bunch of horny pups, got it? I know a lotta ya don't like where this is going. Well neither do I. But an order from the Council is as good as law. Now, Isa and I have been working this for a while and on her request, I bought us some leniencies. You all listen up because anyone who breaks my wishes on this is gonna find themselves in a world of hurt," he essentially barked. He had a good portion of the women behind him now, but still not enough of the more dominant pack members to help keep order.

"No one, and I mean no one, is gonna go out and just grab himself a woman like she's some deli special. This is our pack. All of us. Even the ones not here yet, and you will do well to remember it. I know a lotta you boys are desperate and excited all rolled into one, but you're gonna have about the next two or three hundred years to spend with your mate and treating her like some piece of meat or worse, a breeder, well, that ain't no way to treat your mate and it sure ain't the place I want my own pups grown up in." He had to stop to quell his own resentment before continuing. It was a fat chance he'd ever have a little family of his own and he knew it. There were so few women left; their species was on the verge of extinction. He could have had any female he wanted and she'd have gladly submitted to him, but that was just it. Not only did Rhys think it looked bad for an Alpha to be pulling females away from the omegas, but he was also not even remotely interested in an omega female for his mate.

In truth, a lot of the mating practices of the omegas disgusted him. The males were overly forceful and coercive in choosing their mates and the females just rolled over and took it. It was as if the men were choosing the most defenseless and helpless females, they could find just to stoke their egos, and the women were intentionally weakening themselves just to be more attractive to them. Anytime Rhys tried to make sense of it, he usually just got irritated more. Everything was constantly trying to bring Rhys and his pack down. A female who couldn't hold her own would just be yet another liability for him, and one which he had almost no patience for.

And so, at one hundred and six years old, Rhys was still without a mate. In his mind, he would end up being a bachelor for the rest of his life, and, given the Wylder Pack's obvious intentions, that wouldn't be that much longer anyway.

"What I bought us was time," he continued in his best General Rhys voice. "And I expect you all to use that purchase to do this right. We ain't barbarians; there will no human female turned without her explicit consent and if I find out some idiot took her by force? I'll have his testicles on a platter." Rhys got a little too rough with that one, but he was picturing some mousy little human girl with rape or domination fantasies giving it up to one of the wide-eyed Omega's before him and his stomach was churning at the thought.

"I'm putting Isa in charge of how to go about this. I'm gonna need extra security while this happens though. We need to look after our own and our domain, but the only thing standing between the humans in Riverton and the Wylder Pack is us. Patrols are to use extra caution for the next few years until all this excitement dies down."

"Are they going to start hunting us again?" Inquired a Gamma male in a concerned tone. "I mean, I'm behind ya, Sir, but... once the other packs start grabbing girls from towns... I mean... it just isn't gonna take anyone too long to figure this out and this isn't the dark ages anymore."

There was a general consensus in this concern expressed among the mid-level males and again, Rhys silently swelled with pride. "That's why we've gotta be careful about this," he re-iterated. "We're going to slowly move into the town; fit in and become one of them. We're going to stake our claim to Riverton. Anyone kidnapping women from our town will have hell to pay." Rhys allowed a private and stoic smile to part his lips. "And those girls will never even know that we were up here keeping them safe. I want it to stay that way."

Isa stepped forward then. She was the only one in the tribe with the strength to challenge Rhys's will and almost certainly the only one who could actually remember the dark ages. It was then that she laid out the plan: The younger ones and children born in would get legitimate identities.

Others, like Rhys, would find a way to obtain false paperwork. Everyone, regardless of status, would be expected to get jobs, go to school, to church; whatever it took for the males to put themselves in positions where they would easily meet others.

The integral part of the plan involved the order. In a traditional pack hierarchy, competition for mating occurred at all levels and among both genders, flowing from the top down. It had been that way for centuries. Isa explained to Rhys privately, however, that these human women would not be strong enough to properly defend themselves. Even an Alpha would not have the strengths she required as a human to fight back.

This, of course, was an issue because all of the males would be interested in an alpha female, while only the omegas would be interested in their own.

The wisdom made a great deal of sense to Rhys, too, but for different reasons. If the omegas and other low members were satisfied first, there would be less likelihood for dissent among those ranks. Normally, Rhys wouldn't have cared, but there were considerably more omegas than higher level members in these days. Further, once mated, the omegas would be interested in appearing powerful to their mates. Omegas had a different concept of what that meant; not a one of them would be stupid enough to challenge Rhys or any of the Betas. Instead, that would translate into aggression, which was certainly going to be necessary with the almost certain increase in attacks he expected along their borders.

After the omegas were taken care of, they would move up the ranks in finding mates. With any luck, the omega females would produce some female off-spring, and with that came a chance that one or more was higher. Two omegas could produce an alpha just as easily as two alphas could. There was no rule to it, aside from the knowledge that the higher you moved in rank, the fewer members existed.

At times, Rhys thought about the pack like the military, though that was merely in structure alone. In reality, it was an enormous family; one which Rhys inherited when the last Alphas were killed some 75 ears prior.

The plan seemed like a solid one. With any luck, everyone would follow suit and the pack would be flourishing in no time. Rhys only hoped he could hang on long enough to glimpse the happiness to come... Rhys stepped into his office and hung his hat on the rack. It was going to be a long day. "Captain Forester?" Requested a cordial voice at the door. He turned to look at the office assistant the force had just hired; a young woman named Lily. This was her first internship and the girl was barely out of high school. Surprisingly, she was an excellent worker and Rhys had already started the paper work to recommend hiring her after her internship was finished. "The new files are on your desk, sir," she told him. There was look in her eyes suggesting she wanted to say more, but didn't know how.

"Thank you Ms Campbell," he told her politely. "Was there anything else?" Obviously, there was.

"Well... it's just... I went to high school with Alison..." she stopped, as if she were going to cry.

Rhys offered her as kind of a smile as he could. Kindness simply wasn't his way and the only reason this girl was even talking to him like this, expecting it, was because she had no idea who and what he really was. To her, he was Rhys Forester, Captain of the Police in Riverton. If she knew the reality of things, she'd be screaming for the hills. "Don't worry, darling. We'll find her and get her home safe."

This was the subject of Rhys's long day, and in fact, his long week. It was the first kidnapping in 30 years, since his pack had slowly started moving into Riverton, protecting the population at the same time. They had been wildly successful in their efforts and now nearly a tenth of the town was a part of pack. Once Rhys had been promoted up the ranks of the police force, crime stopped almost completely. The kidnapping did not sit well with him. He knew it wasn't any of his own, and, no one really knew where to start with it.

Lily gave a sweet nod and then turned, leaving Rhys to his long day. The hours drifted by him as he studied the new evidence. It was almost certainly a werewolf. The girl had been snatched when she had gone on a hike in the woods near the house. No ransom. No leads.

"Pardon emua, mi capitan," A tall brown-haired man said at the door, accompanied with a devilish grin. Harvey had always been popular with the ladies and had always been a hopeless romantic to boot. Rhys, however, usually frowned at his antics

Rhys had been deep in thought, reflecting on the pack's growth over the years, and how grateful he was to know that this wasn't done by one of his people. Most of the fervor over the council's ruling to mate with humans had died down by this point, but as Isa and Rhys alike had worried, there had been a sudden peak in kidnappings at the time. Some packs were even rooted out, called cults on the evening news, and large numbers were killed in the process. Naturally, that only hurt the race on the verge of extinction, but it had lessoned some of the external pressures on the pack from the council.

The more it had happened, the more he was grateful for Isa's plan. It kept them out of the public eye. It kept them safe.

"Come in, Harv. I didn't know you were back in town," he commented, extending his hand to greet his younger brother. Harvey and Rhys were very different, and while both demonstrated dominance, Harvey had always, almost naturally, given in to Rhys. Being shorter and less imposing was a factor, of course, but in all honesty, Harvey was more laid back. He could exert dominance when he needed to (and certainly did), but his uncanny ability to shrug off responsibility or worry instantly denied him a position among the alphas.

In their Father's Day, there had been more than one Alpha in the pack. The good times they experienced now were only rivalled by how the pack flourished in that era. Multiple Alphas, however, eventually spelled doom for the pack. Too many leaders with the ability to quickly dissent meant fractioning. When Rhys considered their structure, it more reminded him of the military. The higher you got, the fewer there were until you arrived at the top.

Rhys offered his brother a curious look. "What's goin' on?" He inquired curiously.

Harvey shrugged and grinned in his carefree way. "Eh, don't worry about it. You're busy-"

"Sit down, you old dog," he chuckled at the man. "I need a break from this mess anyway," he added.

Harvey eyed the file with a muted curiosity before Rhys shut it and slid it in a drawer. "Everyone's talking about it,

Rhys," Harvey commented with a nod toward the file. "Was it one of..."

Rhys frowned a bit and nodded for Harvey to pull the door shut. "It wasn't one of ours, but I've got suspicions. Brody said his kids spotted some rogues trying to hunt not far from the den. Can't well put that in here, though can I?" He added, flicking his hand over where he had placed the file. He shook his head. "We'll find her and take care of it," he reassured his brother. "But that's not why you're here, I imagine."

Harvey stifled a grin. "I think I found the one," he said quietly. A chill pushed over Rhys's skin as he heard the words. "In Paris. She's a rogue, but... ooo lala..." Harvey looked up at Rhys's eyes for a brief moment. Eye contact was one of those things that let others know where you stood in the pack. That Harvey could manage the length of time he could was precisely why he was a Beta. "I wasn't going to mate with a human girl, Rhys. I know the council is really eager to see progress, but the thought of that... well, it just wasn't gonna happen," he said with the blunt firmness of a man who was very much in control of himself. "And I know the council's pissed at us for it too but I don't give a damn." Harvey offered his carefree shrug, breaking the eye contact and allowing a grin to smooth the tension. "But I guess it doesn't matter. She's stunning, Rhys."

Rhys cocked an eyebrow. "So, when do we get to meet her?"

"Ah Well... yeah, about that," Harvey started, scratching the back of his neck. "Well, she hasn't fully... I mean... Ah hell, Rhys, she beat the shit out of me," he admitted, sinking slightly in his chair. "I mean, don't get me wrong, I let her win, but... well now she thinks I'm some Gamma or something and isn't interested."

Rhys let out a chuckle but was privately amazed. He'd never met a dominant female, aside from Isa and Starla, a recently born pup, and neither of them were truly in a position to be genuinely combatant with potential suitors' due age. It was a new revelation. He wasn't sure how he felt about it, largely because he was confident that no woman in her right mind would ever try to actually fight Rhys.

Rhys thought for a moment about what he would do. "... and you came back here?" He asked, clearly criticizing his younger brother. "Well no wonder she thinks you're weak, you fool. If she's a true stock, then

I figure every male on the planet has been chasing her tail for the last what, fifty years? What makes you so special?" It was harsh, sure, but something Rhys himself had considered in regards to an Alpha female. It wasn't just about finding her; it was also about whether or not he could win her away from any of the other hundreds of equally desperate Alphas.

Harvey's eyes flared in anger for a moment before he thought about it. "... dear god you're right... what have I done..." His eyes were wide now as they snapped back to Rhys's. Harvey was on his feet, the chair toppling over behind him, in an instant. "I've gotta go back! Shit!"

Harvey was out the door almost as quickly. Rhys rose, adjusted his belt, and lingered in the doorway as he watched the man darting around the precinct toward the nearest exit. Rhys could only chuckle at the scene. Of course, the notion of soul mates was no more true for his kind than it was for humans, but there were all sorts of cultural aspects that made it seem like it was possible sometimes. Males had tremendous honor in courting females. Given their longevity, this courtship could take years, sometimes decades, before they finally paired up. It certainly wasn't instant, love at first sight, as the stories made it out to be.

All the same, humans had lost the formal courtship that the Were's retained and they never had it to the level of the wolves to begin with. Males would fight, but it was not to determine who got the female, as the omegas always misinterpreted. Rather, they were fighting for the females; displaying their power so as to impress her. It was a big distinction. The more dominant the female, the harder she made the males work. But females also fought one another for the same reasons. Additionally, they sometimes fought their suitors, testing their strength themselves.

Rhys had only ever heard of this since the females began to decline shortly after his birth and the situation never improved. Whatever Harvey had gotten himself into would certainly be considered traditional by their standards and Rhys looked forward to the retelling of the event for years to come. For as soft as Harvey appeared, he always managed to get what he wanted and this little French poodle, as Rhys mentally assigned her, was in for a battle with his brother.

"Cap'n Forester?" A voice stirred him from his amusing distraction. Rhys turned to see one of his lieutenants approaching him with a white face.

Rhys frowned, the standard imposing expression setting in naturally. "What's wrong, Officer?"

"Theres... Theres a... Sir I think you'd better come take a look for yourself." The man barely mumbled out.

Frown still present, Rhys followed the man to the only conference room in the precinct. He heard the commotion before he saw the cause.

"- but Ma'am, I already-" Argued one of the officers, an omega in the pack.

"Are you going to keep talking at me or are you going to go get me a white board like I asked?" Came a smooth and terrifyingly confident reply.

The omega's eyes widened and he turned his dismayed expression to Rhys. "Uh... Sir?"

Rhys looked into the conference room. The woman was lithe and toned, wearing a black pencil skirt and four- inch heels. His eyes traced upward until he met her fascinatingly beautiful face. Somewhere inside, something animal-like added that she smelled delightful.

"And who are you?" She interrupted in a commanding tone.

Both of Rhys's eyebrows rose in surprise. He was torn between being intimidated and ripping off both of her arms for the offense. In that moment, he realized he had never actually ever been intimidated by a single person. Concerns sometimes intimidated him, but never individuals. "I am Captain Forester," he replied sharply. He already didn't like where this was heading. "And you are?" "Shepherd," she said, putting down her papers and stepping forward to extend her hand. "Agent Shepherd. You got a notice I was on my way; I assume."

Rhys accepted her hand. Firm grip, brief interaction of touch, no wedding ring. He returned it in kind, but something told him this woman was quite accustomed to being in charge. He used the moment to try and figure out what she was saying. "I'm afraid I didn't get the word. There a reason you're commandeering my conference room, miss?"

"Agent." She corrected in mild irritation. "Agent Shepherd, FBI missing persons," she clarified as she stepped back to the table where she had spread out a lot of files. She tossed her badge at him as her attention moved back to her files. "I am taking over the Alison Reed case and I need the space. You are welcome to call it in to verify my status and affiliation, of course, but in the meantime, I am going to need all of the evidence you've acquired on the case brought in here for review. Case files, too," she added, almost dismissively.

Rhys's mouth would have gone agape were he a lesser man. Instead, he just scowled at her. "Begg'n your pardon, but, like hell you are, Agent," he replied in a commanding way of his own. The other officers gathered around were torn between horrified confusion and passive interest in the exchange. "Lieutenant, go verify Ms. Shephard's badge number, and get ahold of the governor for me too. Ms. Shephard, I'm gonna have to ask you to stop whatever it is you're doing until we can get this cleared up, if that's -"

"Your lack of organization is far from my problem, Captain Forester," she returned smoothly, obviously not taking orders or requests from the man. "I don't have the time to wait for you to sort things out. If busying yourself with useless matters interests you, by all means, go right ahead. Given your rather defensive response, I am going to assume you have interest in this case. If this is true, it is best for Allison and the other girls that you cooperate. Now. The files, Captain, or do I need to have you arrested for obstruction of justice?" Her bright green eyes settled on his with absolutely no intention of moving first.

Rhys decided then that he hated her and wanted to rip her throat out with his teeth. He was no novice at this game. She would move her eyes first if it meant tearing them out himself.

"The local officials will of course be kept in the loop. Your cooperation with this investigation will be invaluable, but I am afraid it has been removed from your jurisdiction. It would be in your best interests to cooperate, Captain," she re-iterated.

"Sir?"

"WHAT?" Rhys barked in reply.

"Badge number checks out, sir. The governor requests our department's full cooperation with miss, I mean, Agent Shepherd's investigation."

Rhys rolled his eyes before he realized what he had done. He broke off contact first. Dominance was hers.

"Thank you, Lieutenant," she called over his shoulder. "Now, Captain, I am afraid I cannot entertain any further delays. Those files, if you would be so kind," she instructed in an all business tone as she sat down and returned to her files.

Rhys stepped forward into the conference room, veritably slamming the door shut behind him. "What other girls." He demanded, his face starting to grow red from the fury he was experiencing.

Agent Shepherd rolled her eyes and then looked at him seriously, again, straight in the eyes. "Three girls. Three different towns all along the river. All three were kidnapped under similar conditions with no ransom efforts made," she explained tersely. She paused for a moment, seemingly to assess him. "Are we done comparing dicks now, Captain? Because there is a lot of ground that needs to be covered and it's likely that your search parties are looking in the wrong place." No one in his entire life had ever dared speak to him with such disregard. She was like an alpha male neatly packaged in the body of a tiny little woman.

His blood boiled and he genuinely considered shifting just to put her in her place. Finally, he broke the eye contact again to throw the door open. "GET ME THE REED FILES!" He bellowed at his terrified staff.

He returned to the agent and sat down with a grimacing frown mixed with embarrassment as a gamma brought the requested files. If he had to guess, they had drawn straws and the most dominant male available ended up volunteering to interface with him. Only the wolves among them actually understood what would happen if Rhys lost control. It hadn't been more than a few decades since his last kill, but the way he had ripped the throat from the arrogant rogue who threatened a campsite near Riverton was enough to pale even his betas. Rhys was fierce in how he defended his pack and their territory. The success of Isa's plan to keep them out of trouble only made it worse.

Shepherd was not at all impressed, but she wasn't stupid either. She knew she needed the help of the locals if their search parties were to stand a chance. "I can't have helicopters here until next week. This place is fairly isolated. All searches will have to happen on foot unless you know of someone willing to provide air support. The agency will of course refund their time and fuel."

"What are the conditions of the other kidnappings," Rhys replied, completely ignoring her suggestion. "I haven't heard about this," he included before thinking about it.

Shepherd cocked her eyebrow at him. "Obviously. I am really quite appalled at the lack of communication these communities have with one another. Might be why they are targeting this area, though," she offered.

That caught his attention and for the second time since he had met her, the hair on the back of his neck stood up. "They?"

Shepherd looked mildly irritated. "This is confidential. I needn't explain how disclosing this information could negatively impact the outcome of this investigation, I would hope. The Agency is of the opinion that Ms. Reed's kidnapping, along with the other three young women, is a part of a larger scale action. About thirty years ago, we became aware of a cult of massive size and infrastructure. Until then, we assumed it a series of individual cults but once the kidnappings began, well we were made aware that each one was in fact a unit of a larger organization. The kidnappings all follow the same MO: The girl is isolated in the woods and disappears. No ransom, no tangible leads, few witnesses. All of the girls are between the ages of 16 and 21. They share similar appearances, personalities, and dispositions. Often times, all we find are the shredded remains of whatever clothing she was wearing the day of the crime."

Rhys had paled. For all their efforts to stay out of this, it had come to them none the less. Worse, Shepherd was extremely intelligent. He gathered that after the first few minutes of interaction. She was going to put all of the pieces together and expose his pack. That the woman was a threat was making it harder to resist killing her outright. The only thing holding him back was her position in the human hierarchy.

"The Bureau rooted out a few of the larger cells some 25 years ago. It has uncovered smaller cells periodically

"The Bureau rooted out a few of the larger cells some 25 years ago. It has uncovered smaller cells periodically since and it is always due to one of their members getting sloppy in a kidnapping. This is why the agency has become involved with this case. Chances are high that there is a cult operating out of the forest of this area which means there are likely four times as many girls being held there against their will as what has been reported."

Rhys didn't know what to do. "Well a cult is a little beyond my means of handling," he told her in an unsure voice. Let her think I'm intimidated by the information, he told himself.

Shepherd gave him an analyzing look for a moment. "We'll need all missing persons reports for the last thirty years," she told him flatly.

"You're looking at them," he answered with a nod toward the Reed file.

Shepherd cocked a skeptical eyebrow. "She's the first? In thirty years. Really." Shepherd did not believe him in the slightest, in spite of the fact that it was quite true. "Must be a real quiet place to live."

Rhys shrugged it off, still looking concerned. "We got our share of crime. Riverton is a small town, Agent. Not a lot of traffic." An idea hit him just then. He might be able to put her on the same track he was. It was safer that way and would eliminate the threat to the pack. "You don't... you don't suppose this cult of yours is trying to move in, do you? Some sorta transient types?"

Shepherd lifted her eyebrows in consideration and internally, Rhys was celebrating. "This area certainly matches the demographics they prefer. Isolated, heavily wooded, lots of... I should warn you, Captain, that this cult has some rather disturbing customs."

"Yeah, well, kidnapping young women is pretty disturbing enough, ma'am," he commented through a snort.

"They eat raw meat and prefer it fresh. At first, we believed that the young women were some sort of virgin sacrifice. Later we learned their fate was more... carnal... in nature and less motivated by some sort of religious fervor. So, you'll understanding the point of my question when I ask what sort of game your local hunters are bringing in?"

Rhys met her eyes straight on this time. "Elk, mostly. Lotta dear too," he answered.

"What about your predator population? Mountain lions? Bears? Wolves?" She continued fluidly.

"All of the above," he answered. "Why?"

"The cult often attempts to cover their tracks by making the abductions appear to be an animal attack. Generally speaking, they prefer wolves as their cover of choice. Obviously, it makes a lot more sense in an area where such predators exist naturally, ergo their attraction to this location. Seen a lot more wolves than you are used to lately, Captain?"

Rhys saw his singular opportunity to get this cleaned up without jeopardizing his pack. "Yeah," he said with a surprised nod. "Hunters been taking them out of the hills for weeks now," he added for good measure. "I didn't think it was related..."

Shepherd shrugged it off. "Most don't. That's the point. I'm going to need to request you redirect your search parties to the areas where the wolves have been spotted. And that air support, Captain?"

"I'll see what I can get together," he acquiesced. "But I'm gonna need some more information on these people if I'm sending my volunteers into those hills," he added. He needed to know what she knew about werewolves, even if she didn't realize that's what she was dealing with.

Shepherd was tired of interruptions. "They are exceptionally strong," she told him frankly. "Most experts on the matter believe that the high protein diet is a factor. They will be young men between the ages of 18 and 30, various racial backgrounds. They also will have trained wolves with them. For a shock effect, many of the young men do not wear clothing either. Animal traps have proven effective in the past for dealing with the wolves." She offered the last part without blinking an eye. Inside, Rhys was cringing at such brutal techniques.

"Well, I'll let them know then. And I'll let you know how the search goes," he added.

"No need, Captain," she answered, folding her file shut and pulling her jacket from behind the chair. "I am participating in the effort."

Rhys offered her a chuckle. It was all he could do to keep from cringing further. "Begging your pardon, ma'am, but this isn't the city. You'll snap an ankle in those," he said with a nod toward her 4-inch heels. He tried his best to make it sound as condescending as possible. She was dressed for a power meeting in time square, not a search party in western Wyoming.

Shepherd rolled her eyes at him and offered a smirk; the first half effort at a smile since she arrived. She was really quite pretty. "Oh, don't you worry your sweet little head over me, dear," she replied with precisely the same tone. His mental image revived the notion of ripping her arms off. Shepherd crossed over to a small duffle bag slung over the back of a chair. She swung the bag over her shoulder before round the table for the door. "The women's dressing room, captain?" She inquired as she passed him on the way out the door.

"Down the hall to your right," he told her through a frown. She signaled that she got it and soon disappeared. The lieutenant joined him from behind, still looking bewildered about her presence. "Watch her," was the only order Rhys spared the man. It was so deathly serious; he might as well have been another person.

A few minutes later, Agent Shepherd emerged from the changing room wearing jeans, sneakers, and a zip up sweater with the words "Princeton" displayed across the chest in bold letters. She was tugging on a rain jacket and holding her badge in her teeth as she left. On her hip was a holstered Glock. Rhys hadn't told her that they were about to begin their next wave of searches, though, she seemed to already know.

Agent Shepherd snagged a map as she turned and left the precinct, presumably heading toward her car. Rhys thoroughly regretted what he was about to say, but knew there was little another alternative. "You need a ride, Agent?" He offered, torn about how he wanted her to respond.

The woman stopped and looked at him for a moment. She seemed to be torn about the same thing. "Yeah, I guess," she finally let out. Shepherd was, of course, weighing her options. The Bureau's position was that she was to take her own vehicle and remain as separate from the locals as possible. Of course, with the amount of ground they had to cover, there was no way it would happen without the local's assistance. So long as she could remind Captain Forester that she was in charge, and not him anymore, being sociable with him and his could work to her benefit in eliciting cooperation.

She hopped into the beat-up old truck and pulled the door shut without another word, busying herself with her seat belt as Rhys hopped into the driver's side. The other police cars were following suit, waiting to follow the Captain's beat up truck.

"So," Rhys finally said after several minutes of deafening silence. "Princeton."

Shepherd cocked an eyebrow at him, trying to pretend that she was involved in her case files. In truth, reading in the bumpy vehicle was making her car sick and she would never admit that the idle conversation was a welcomed remedy. "Yeah. What about it," she answered non-committal.

"Awfully fancy school," Rhys responded with the same level of enthusiasm. "You join the Bureau straight away or did you do any real work first?" He hadn't meant it as it came out and he cringed slightly on the inside. This already was starting poorly and he needed her to think he was cooperating completely for his idea to pull through.

"Real work, huh?" She replied. He expected as much. "No, I don't suppose you would consider graduate work at an ivy league institution to be real work, would you Captain?"

"Sorry," he retreated a bit. Agent Shepherd couldn't have known that he had only ever apologized to a handful of people in his life, sincere or otherwise. "Didn't mean it to sound like that. What'd you study?" "No offense taken," she replied smoothly. "I studied criminal justice, specializing in the occult."

"Then you're something' of an expert about these folks who you think made off with Alison? You ever see one of 'em?" Rhys was mildly curious. Humans wouldn't know it, necessarily, but once you knew what to look for, there were defining physical characteristics which all werewolves shared.

Agent Shepherd shook her head, which oddly came as a relief to Rhys. "Most of the extractions and raids happened when I was just a kid," she told him. Rhys bit his lip slightly.

Age with humans was always hard for him to figure out. He had guessed she was probably in her early twenties, but hearing that she was an FBI agent and now some sort of academic as well meant she was likely a lot older than that initial estimate. "There was one near my home town, actually," she revealed. "That's how I got interested."

"I get it," he answered, nodding slightly. "Gotta taste of something' bad and felt helpless so now it's your life's goal to make sure it doesn't happen again?" He was thinking out loud, really, and, not really thinking at all.

"Something like that," she said dismissively. "Your files on the Reed girl don't indicate that anyone has interviewed her friends," she changed the subject rapidly. Apparently, he hit a nerve.

"Girl didn't have many," he answered.

"She'd have had at least one," Shepherd countered. "A sister, maybe? Best friend? These girls are quiet types and extremely private. They tend to fly under the radar. Many of them aren't noticed missing for days after they are taken; it's part of the reason they are selected."

"That's sad," Rhys commented absently. He meant it, too. Suddenly, he wondered about the girls who had joined the pack in the last thirty years. "Selected, huh. Like these fellas are stalking these girls beforehand?"

"Something like that," she answered.

"See, I figure we'd have noticed some strange naked boys running around watching girls. Maybe we're just a bunch of amateurs."

Shepherd rolled her eyes and scoffed at him. "Well I would hope you would have noticed that," she answered in full sarcasm. "They like to remain hidden. They would probably be lurking in the woods right in front of you and wouldn't even know it. Given how easily they manage this; I seriously doubt any inexperience you or your force may be dealing with has anything to do with it."

"They're just that good, huh?" Rhys continued. "Then why'd they send only one of you and not a whole crew?"

"Don't worry, Captain Forester," she replied in a smooth and utterly condescending voice. "You and your men will get all the credit you're due. I am simply here to guide the investigation and provide insight in the event it's the cult. You'll have plenty of opportunity to get your hands dirty."

The truck pulled off the road into a small gravel turn off. Shepherd had been tapping at her phone with a frown for the last several miles. "Don't get no signal out here," Rhys told her curtly.

Shepherd had a sour look on her face for a moment, but decided to put the phone away anyway. She stepped out of the truck to where the others had gathered, momentarily pausing to take in the environment. Under any other circumstance, this place would have been stunningly beautiful. Tall ponderosa pines blanketed the mountain for miles, unblemished by civilization. The heavy smell of pine tar hung in the air as her sneakers crunched on the soft, needle covered ground beneath her feet. A dense fog had settled over the valleys and with the exception of a few stray birds, and a rather irritated squirrel, the vast wilderness was oddly quiet.

Shepherd only took a minute to assess the place. She stepped over to where the men were gathered, instantly flashing her badge. "Agent Shepherd, FBI," she announced, preparing to pull out the map.

"FBI?" Let out one man in surprise. "Well, hell, I didn't know we was that important?" It was Jameson, one of the pack omegas. All of the search party were wolves from the Forester Pack. There was no way Rhys was taking volunteers who couldn't handle what was out there.

Shepherd ignored him. "Intel on the people responsible suggests a certain preference toward locations, here, here, and here, " she said, circling the best possible locations with a red sharpie. Naturally, one of them was the Den's main house. Shepherd was good. Very good. "I suggest we focus on these three areas first. Are there any natural cave formations in any of these areas?"

Rhys shook his head. This was, of course, a lie. One of those locations did have a natural cave; his den. That she was able to identify quality wolf habitats, though, was rather of interest to him. They hadn't considered looking in places they themselves would like, and even if they didn't find anything, after she left it gave the pack alternative hunting and living grounds in the case of an emergency or if the Den were ever discovered.

Shepherd had just proven valuable, as far as his pack was concerned, and his internal beast relaxed on seeing her as a threat.

"Fine," she answered, "I would have expected there to be some, but ok. My research indicates that this location here is the best starting point, barring any caves or cave systems." It was not the Den and everyone discretely relaxed. "We should start there, fan out, and meet back here in six hours to report. Does everyone have radios?"

"Ma'am, radios don't work too good out here. Hills mess 'em up," another omega, Micah, chimed in. "But we got a good way we worked out few days back. Just whistle really loud like this," Micah demonstrated, not at all realizing how critical Shepherd's expression had become. To Rhys, it was obvious: she thought Micah was a complete idiot. Fortunately, she masked the expression well enough.

Rhys was mildly embarrassed, but also had come prepared. "Might be easier with these," he commented absently, pulling out a handful of police issued whistles. Shepherd seemed less opposed to the notion and the others were visibly rather excited to receive the item.

The group spread out, though Rhys did not let Shepherd out of his sight. He was largely worried that she would accidentally stumble upon evidence of his own pack, instantly make the connection, and then turn that fancy Glock on her hip against one of his family. For a city girl, she was handling herself well in the rough terrain.

Mostly, the group was silent as they trekked along and it wasn't until Shepherd slipped on a wet rock that Rhys had any reason to interact with her. Before he had even considered it, his hand shot out to latch onto her arm, preventing the spill by pulling her up slightly. The woman stumbled a bit more and ultimately ended up fully embraced in Rhys's grip. A flutter raced through Rhys's heart and his keen senses noticed that her own pulse had elevated. She smelled like lavender and woman and the scent of her immediately caught his attention as unique.

Rhys frowned instantly. In reality, he hadn't expected such a response and it only served to confuse him. "Better watch your step there, Ma'am," he grumbled as he let go of her arms and turned to continue his search.

"...yeah," she returned, in much the same grouchy tone as he had used with her. "I think we are getting off baring," she piped up.

"What makes you think that?" He called back in disinterest. He knew they were; that was part of the plan. He needed to keep them away from the pack. He would send Brody and his team to scout this area later; the formality of this search party was merely to appease Agent Shepherd and possibly acquire information to aid Brody later.

"Because we're heading too far south," she replied, pulling out her compass to verify what she seemed to already know. "We need to double back at the top of that ridge. Don't suppose you have some way of whistling that to your buddies, do you?"

Rhys shook his head. "You and I can head back that way and then meet back up with them at the rendezvous if you're interested." He was hoping she was not.

"I guess," she answered, already adjusting her heading as she continued up the hill toward the ridge. "I suppose we're still in ear shot for these whistles of yours," she added. "Were you able to ascertain when Miss Reed was abducted? The case file said it was in the evening but I did not notice a specific time."

"Your cult only kidnaps girls at certain times?" He asked, genuinely a little confused.

"Of course not," Shepherd replied as if the notion was absurd. "It does tend to be near full moons, but we suspect it has more to do with night time visibility than any mythos associated with it. Not like we're dealing with werewolves or something here," she added with a chuckle. It was a good thing that Rhys was walking in front of her or else she'd have seen him go white with the comment.

By the time the pair made it to the crest, Rhys realized that they were indeed well out of ear shot. It made him more uncomfortable to wonder if his omegas would potentially miss something than it did to consider that anything might happen to him or the agent here on this ridge. "Don't see anything here," Rhys announced in his usual no nonsense tone. "We should head back."

Shepherd was frowning. "Come take a look at this," Shepherd replied sternly. The woman had bent over and was examining fresh tracks in the mud. "Have you ever seen a print this big?" She asked, almost to herself. It was a wolf print, but no ordinary one; a werewolf print.

Rhys frowned. Judging by the size, it was an alpha male. There were others nearby which clearly made up the rest of this rogue pack that had invaded his territory. The alpha male was likely to be comparable in size to Rhys. This was not a welcomed discovery. "No," he replied without thinking about it. "Looks like a wolf track though."

Shepherd looked up at him, indicating that she had paled. Internally Rhys felt a bit of vindication to see her intimidated, though he himself was too pre-occupied with the implications of her discovery to truly appreciate it. "I'm sorry, Captain. I think the cult is here." Shepherd pushed to her feet and started jogging down the hill to where they should have gone to begin with. "We've got to find the girl and fast before they do something to her."

"Wait, what?" Rhys replied, bordering on angry. "Do what to her? You left that part out!"

"No shit, Sherlock," Shepherd replied as she raced down the hill, her eyes darting every which way to absorb as much of the landscape as she could in hopes of finding a trace of the missing girl. Rhys turned sour at the remark. "I didn't want to concern you in the event that this did not turn out to be the cult, and, I didn't want to effect the investigation. They have some sort of chemical or something that they use on the girls. Makes them believe they are actually animals or something. I've never seen a rescued girl cured from whatever they do to her." "Is it contagious?" Rhys yelled after her. He of course already knew it was. He also knew it wasn't a chemical so much as a hormone with almost parasitic-like characteristics. It was a chemical found in the saliva of all were's and it took a full month before it completely turned a human. Shepherd's comment about the full moons providing light was entirely correct. Night time hunts were easier with that light source in place and in ancient times, this was when rogue's often hunted humans. If the human survived, he or she would experience his or her first turning exactly one month later; on another full moon. Thus, the mythos was born.

"Only if they bite you," she replied as she slid down an embankment to a glade approaching a creek. Rhys was right behind her, intent on yelling at her, when he picked up the scent. Three wolves were in this area and none of them were his own.

Shepherd's face contorted slightly. "Something's not right..." she muttered to herself as she slowly pulled her hand gun.

Rhys's frown mirrored hers. You're damn straight, he thought dismally, now wondering how he was going to protect Shepherd, fight these rogues, and keep the Agent from figuring out anything else in the process. It seemed hopeless. Following suit, Rhys pulled his revolver, albeit non-committal. He had a much more effective way of dealing with this particular threat than a gun. "Don' suppose I'm needing silver bullets?" He whispered to her half-heartedly.

Agent Shepherd frowned and held up a hand to silence him. Again, Rhys's inner wolf growled dangerously at this presumptuous woman. Mixed with her scent from before, he was now torn between tearing out her gut or bending her over. Neither option was acceptable and it only served to frustrate Rhys further.

The pair quietly crept along until they stopped at an abandoned camp-site. The rogues had heard them coming and left the vicinity. Likely, they picked up on Rhys's scent before that and were long gone. Shepherd's tension did not abate, however, she did re-holster her gun as she examined the camp-site. It was nothing more than a hastily extinguished fire pit and some abandoned camp gear from a bygone era.

Rhys was too busy scanning the woods around them to even take notice of the camp. He had definitely picked up three wolves, but they had moved too quickly to have had Allison with them and he wasn't sure he had scented any females either. If they had been Alphas, they'd have stayed and fought Rhys. In a way, their behavior only made him bolder and he swallowed the desire to shift and chase after the cowards.

As he turned back, Rhys saw Agent Shepherd stooping and examining a locket. Her face had gone deathly white and for the moment, she was unaware of anything but it. "What's that?" Rhys asked gruffly, harshly re-holstering his revolver.

"A locket..." She replied, as if she were in a dream. "It... it was my sister's...."

"Dad?" Analise's voice cracked slightly as she sat on the edge of the bed in the hotel in Riverton. She was idly thumbing the locket that she and Captain Forrester had found earlier that day while she phoned her father back in Boston.

Rhys had said nothing to her after she found the necklace and had actually been rather accommodating for the instant silence that followed as Analise Shepherd sank into her own memories. In truth, she felt foolish and she knew her case was going to suffer because of it.

"... Just kidding. Obviously, I'm not around, so do your thing after the beep."

Analise's heart sunk a little further. How long had it been since she had called her parents that she didn't even realize her dad had a prank voice mail recording on his cell phone...

"Hey Dad," she spoke into the phone with a sweet tone that would have caused Rhys to do a double take. "Real funny. Hey, uhm... could you or mom give me a call? I'm out in the sticks so if you don't get through leave a message and I'll call you when I get it. I uh.... I miss you dad. Talk to you later."

She almost sounded like a different person and a part of that made Analise uncomfortable. The tension between her and her parents had been brewing for years, starting with when Laura had gone missing.

The event changed her. She was only five when it happened, but Analise clearly remembered the day as the one her childhood died. From that point on, her entire life had become devoted to finding the bastards that had snatched her sister away. Everything from her choice in college to the books she read pertained to this, and frankly, it exhausted her. Agent Shepherd had never had the life she had wanted. No boyfriends, which meant no husband, no children, no friends, nothing. She had given up everything with the singular hope of finding some justice for Laura.

A knock on the door pulled Analise out of her own misery. Without thinking, she quickly wiped the stray tears that had formed and tossed her cell phone into her purse while making sure her Glock was out and easy to grab if need be. "Just a second," she called at the door before giving it another thought. "Who's there?" She added, her tone having returned to normal.

"It's Rhys." Came the gruff, no-nonsense announcement, muffled by the door.

Shepherd frowned as she opened the door. "Are there any developments?" She asked.

Rhys cocked his eyebrow skeptically at her. Analise hadn't changed out of her jeans or zip up hoody and dressed like this, he could almost see himself being able to relate to her. Almost. "Nice to see you too," he answered dryly.

CHAPTER 2

Analise was not amused and simply cocked her eyebrow in return as a response.

"No. No new developments," Rhys told her through a sigh. "Team searched that campsite but they didn't find anything." His piercing blue eyes settled easily on hers in yet another staring match. "Why didn't you tell me?" Came his firm demand.

Analise let out a tired sigh and closed her eyes to steady herself. She was definitely not in the mood for this. Rhys took her eye closing as a victory and had to muffle a smirk at the corners of his lips. "Look... You're right. I should have told you that they use poisons but honestly, I figured it would do more harm than good. Scaring people away is the last thing we need given how much area is still unexplored."

"Wasn't talking about that," Rhys concluded with a nod to her hand, still holding onto the necklace.

Analise bristled and took on an even more stern expression than Rhys thought possible. "Because it's none of your business?" She answered in an attempt to point out how rude she thought he was.

"Sure as hell is my business if it affects your job," Rhys countered firmly. "We're just a small no-never mind town to a big shot like you. Some of the men out there searching for Allison are my family. Now, I'm not looking for you to bare your heart or -- "

"That's good, Captain Forrester, because this conversation is over. If you are concerned about my professional performance, I am more than happy to provide you a DPO you can file with the headquarter office at the capital. Is there anything else?"

"Yeah, how old was she?" Rhys continued, completely unphased by Shepherd's all business tone. He wasn't sure why he wanted to know and suddenly regretted even asking. Somewhere beneath her icy, stand-offish exterior was a young woman in pain. Still he didn't know why he even cared. Lots of people were in pain; what made her so special?

Analise dropped her head into her hand and chuckled to herself. "You are unbelievable," she muttered, still smirking in deprecation. "Heh, fine. What the hell. Her name was Laura. She's my older sister. They kidnapped her from the woods outside our house almost thirty years ago. She was fifteen at the time. I was five. Kinda sorta worshiped the ground she walked on. That is why I joined the Bureau. That is the personal tragedy that thrust me into this career. Any other personal facts you'd like to demand knowledge of, Rhys? Wanna know my favorite color or the name of my cat?"

Rhys's jaw went tight as he pictured himself slugging the woman in the jaw. He was never violent to women and only violent with men if it was a were threatening his territory, but this woman certainly challenged his self-restrained.

"I was gonna express my condolences but maybe I should just get going," Rhys turned to leave and then, his emotions got the best of him and he spun around, fully prepared for a battle. "You... I... Damn it, woman, you know it wouldn't kill you to be a little more... more... more human every now and then!"

Rhys suddenly questioned what he just said. Who was he to lecture her on humanity?

Analise had been prepared for a battle, as had Rhys, but his Question only served to disarm her. The edges of her lips curled slightly into an amused grin that in turn frustrated Rhys further. "You know, Captain, I've been terrible rude," she answered genuinely. Rhys's expression indicated what she assumed would happen. Analise and kind were two words that scarcely seemed to go together and pretty much everyone was stunned when they did.

"I appreciate your concern, but no, my sister's murder isn't going to affect me on this one. If anything, I will be more interested in catching these assholes than usual, given their obvious connection with her disappearance." She folded her arms across her chest and took a deep breath, not once breaking eye contact. Analise, apparently, was just about as good at apologies as Rhys was.

Rhys sighed heavily, all of his frustration now having no outlet. "Damn city folk," he muttered under his breath. "Well, I am sorry for your loss." In truth, he really was. Rhys had fought for decades to ensure that no woman in their neck of the woods would ever have to endure what Laura did at the hands of werewolves' hell bent on finding breeders. "But I am glad to hear your dedication to resolving this case."

It was an awkward moment of silence after that. Rhys had really stretched for a reason to visit her. After she so easily found the Rogue campsite, he was rather concerned about what she would uncover if she went snooping at any of the other locations she had circled on that little map of hers, and he decided it would be better if she were supervised for the rest of her stay.

Naturally, none of the police force were wanted anything to do with her. Analise had an uncanny way of intimidating everyone she came in contact with.

"Well. I guess I'll see you in the morning."

Analise nodded once. "Yep," she replied, slowly closing her door.

Rhys was frustrated again as he returned to his beat up old chevy. His scowl hadn't left even well after he pulled into the gravel parking lot of the den. Isa was already waiting for him outside with her hands folded gently in her lap as she slowly rocked in the wooden rocking chair. Isa was impressive, and not merely due to her longevity. Among were's, living to be over 700 was completely unheard of and Rhys often figured that the only reason the Wylders, or any other pack for that matter, hadn't tried to destroy them was because of the respect Isa brought them. Even the elders on the council stopped and listened to her sage-like advice.

And so, when the old woman offered him the distant expression of a wise old woman, he wasn't terribly surprised. "Her scent lingers on you still," Isa replied flatly as Rhys started to walk by. It was sufficient for him to stop dead in his tracks.

"Wha... who's scent?" He inquired curiously.

"The human woman who will haunt us," Isa answered, only now looking up to offer Rhys a critical look. "She is powerful and her blood is ideal for mixing with ours." That was Isa's way of saying that the Lycan virus wouldn't kill Analise; it would convert her. "Some of the men are concerned. She is this era's version of a Werewolf hunter and she has found our den. Those with pups are speaking of fleeing. There is great fear in our pack. What will you do?"

Rhys let out a heavy sigh as he slid down the side of the building to sit on the ground next to her rocker. "Hell if I know," he said, the frown seemingly permanently affixed to his face. "And there's a small pack of rogues around too. I didn't get a whiff of whether or not the missing girls with them. I suspect she is. Agent Shepherd said there's three others who've been grabbed too. This is spinning out of control..."

Isa frowned. "Will the human woman leave if the girl is found?"

Rhys shrugged, thought for a moment, and then shook his head. "Probably not. By the sounds of it, the rogue pack kidnapped her older sister back when the decree came out. Thirty years is a pretty long time to hold a grudge. She's built her whole life around rooting out dens as some form of revenge or justice or both and now she caught wind of the guys who nabbed her sister?" Rhys chuckled at his own misfortune. "No, she'll stay and finish the job. I know I would if I were in her shoes."

A picture of four inch heels and perfectly toned legs splashed vibrantly before Rhys's eyes. He shook away the mental image of Agent Shepherd's figure and tried to replace the thoughts with his hands throttling her neck. She was mind bogglingly irritating and apparently more dangerous than even he had considered, but she was also wildly attractive and he had yet to vent all the pent up aggression her arrogance and defiance was stirring inside.

Isa returned her distant gaze forward. "Then your choice is simple," she stated. "You must either turn her or kill her."

Rhys turned an alarmed look at Isa for such a brutal decision, but ultimately said nothing. Isa was probably right, of course, as always. Shepherd was a threat; probably a greater one than all the alpha and beta males in the Wylder pack combined. He wondered for a moment how many happy families she had destroyed by raiding dens. How many alphas would kill just to be in this position, after what she had personally done to their respective packs?

The alarm morphed into rage and his fists clenched down a little harder. Of course Isa was right. But then, it was not as simple as she made it sound. There was the problem of Analise's status. Rhys frowned slightly. "Can't kill her," he commented in the same nonchalant tone Isa was employing. "She's too important in the human hierarchy; someone would come looking for her and then we'll have the whole town crawling with agents just as talented as her."

"Then you have your solution," Isa concluded with a nod. "Whatever you chose, do it quickly. We cannot risk what is transpiring around us."

Rhys offered an agreeing grunt as he pushed himself up, heading inside to what was sure to be panic and pandemonium. Oh what he wouldn't give to abandon this sort of responsibility to someone else...

Before he had a chance to storm off to the privacy of his own apartment, Brody, the most dominant of the betas stepped in his path. "We need to talk," Brody stated in his deep baritone.

Rhys didn't think his frown could get worse. "You didn't find the pack," he more stated than asked.

"No, but that's small potatoes. Micah just called. Apparently four of ours just got into a fight at the bar and your little girlfriend arrested all of 'em. They want you down at the drunk tank."

Rhys was torn between lunging at Brody for implying any sort of relationship between him and Shepherd and ordering the beta to slaughter all four men who would be stupid enough to pull a stunt like that with an FBI agent so obviously sniffing around. Rhys's jaw tightened in anger as he spun back around, storming his way out of the den and back toward the beat up chevy. Brody trotted along behind him.

"Where the fuck you think you're going?" Rhys snarled at him, unable to restrain his frustration any longer.

"One of 'em's a gamma and they're all drunk off their rockers," Brody replied curtly as he pulled open the passenger door and hopped inside. "Figure you'll need some help if we're gonna do this without shifting. Unless you don't care about that."

"God damn that woman," Rhys hissed as he jammed the keys into the ignition and slammed his foot down on the gas, sending the back tires spinning and kicking gravel all over the parking lot. "I should just kill her and be done with this."

Brody cocked an eyebrow. "Yeah, she sounds like a threat. Boys have been yammering all day about her."

"I'll take care of it," Rhys answered hotly. "What did you find at the rogue's campsite?" "Whole lotta nothing'," Brody answered. "There were some tracks up the hill about a quarter mile. A male and a two females at the camp, definitely more in the woods around the area. Shifted at the crest and took off as humans by the look of things. Wandered back around where your search parties were looking so we would lose the tracks. Seemed to work, too. So far, with what Jameson and Micah spotted on our hunt earlier, I'd say we're dealing with about ten of them."

"TEN?!" Shouted Rhys. "You can't find ten sloppy rogues in our own woods after that bitch literally drew you a fucking map?!"

Brody's eyes averted slightly at this. "We're working on it best we can, boss," he answered as if his tail were tucked between his legs. "And they sure as hell aren't sloppy. They've been covering their tracks like pros; walking in lines and whatnot to hide their numbers. This ain't normal. Hell, I wouldn't be surprised if these folks came from the Council."

Rhys was not in the mood to coddle Brody's injured ego with this one. There were two threats working against them. Rhys was trusting Brody to handle the rogues, expecting it of him, in fact. "We'll go on a hunt for them tonight and end this now," Rhys said in a gravelly serious voice as the hair on his hands and arms began to thicken and raise. With a displeased growl, Rhys swallowed back the inadvertent starts of a shift to his hybrid form. It had been 75 years since he'd been angry enough to shift without meaning to.

"Fine," Brody muttered, obviously humiliated that Rhys had to step in to help him.

The truck took the turn sharply, causing the tires to screech against the pavement as Rhys brought the old pick up to a jerking stop. Both Rhys and Brody were out of the vehicle in seconds, each slamming the door angrily as they left. Rhys was rather surprised the old beast had stood up to so much abuse over the years and silently promised the vehicle that he'd make it up to her.

The pair trotted into the precinct to enter into the chaos ensuing there. Agent Shepherd was in the conference room barking orders into her cell phone while three of the four in the drunk tank were taking turns howling like wolves. The evening skeleton crew was running around like chickens without their heads, either attempting to calm down the energetic drunks or trying to talk down Shepherd, who was doing an excellent job ignoring them.

Rhys let out a small sigh at the scene. "We're fucked," Brody muttered under his breath. Rhys turned to regard him with a half-hearted smirk. He had pretty much summed it all up.

"Alright," he said, clapping Brody on the back. "You take care of those idiots. I'll handle the devil woman."

Brody chuckled and jogged back to the drunk tank, obviously shouting at the fools and trying to get a grip on this situation. Meanwhile, Rhys walked over to the conference room just as Shepherd had kicked out the remainder of the staff and locked the door. He rolled his eyes. Had to make it hard on him, didn't she?

Rhys knocked on the door, exercising as much restraint as he physically could. "Agent Shepherd, it's Captain Forrester. Open the door."

There was a pause, during which time Rhys considered just breaking the damned thing off its hinges, before Analise threw it open and glared furiously at him. The woman was a mess. She had a bruised cheek that would almost certainly turn into an impressive black eye and a split lip. Her clothes were torn, blood stained, and disheveled. It had been one hell of a fight.

Rhys offered her a genuinely surprised look. "What the fuck happened to you?" He let out without thinking about it.

"Nice peaceful little community, he says. Hardly any crime at all, he says. Bull fucking shit," she retorted furiously. "You listen here, asshole," she continued in such dominant aggression that Rhys actually considered backing away with his hands up. Suddenly, he felt badly for laying into Brody on their drive here. This seemed to be a taste of his own medicine. "I don't give a shit what sort of corrupt district you're running here, but you are obviously withholding information on undocumented crime statistics that could have pertinence to this investigation and if you think I'm gonna let that shit fly, you're in for Suite the surprise. You have no fucking idea what you are dealing with!"

Rhys was alarmed for the briefest of moments. No one in his entire life had ever spoken to him like this and it was only serving to provoke a challenging reaction out of him. If Analise knew how close she was to watching a werewolf shift before her very eyes, she likely would have shut her mouth.

Yep. Gonna have to kill her, he told himself in sardonic humor. In reality, he Questioned whether or not it was wise to turn someone with this degree of dominance. It was alarming even by wolf standards and worse, Analise was obviously holding back too. He was pretty sure he didn't want to see her as a pissed off wolf.

The true intimidation and challenge Rhys experience lasted only a moment. He rolled his eyes and latched onto her wrist, tugging her out of the conference room.

"Your nose is still bleeding there, killer," he commented, which completely disarmed her momentarily as she paused to inspect. He took a couple of steps before depositing her in an office chair and stepping over to the mini fridge to pull out a frozen rib eye. "Ok," he said pushing her hand away as he placed the meat on her swelling cheek. His other hand cupped behind her head, to get a good amount of pressure on the injury. Much to his surprise and dismay, the move served to arouse them both. Had he been anything other than a werewolf, the scent of her arousal would have been her little secret. For a pissed off alpha, however, she may as well shove it up his nose. For the second time that day, he decided that she smelled delightful, and, for the second time that day, that realization only further angered him.

"Now you're gonna calm your pretty little ass down and start telling me what the hell just happened here or I'm gonna toss your ass in the drunk tank with your new friends and let you all sort this out like big kids, got it?"

Analise offered him an unamused glare as her jaw tightened. She had, in fact, calmed down and pushed the offending rib eye away. "Seriously, what the hell sort of police department has frozen steaks on hand?" She inquired in an irritated sarcasm. At least she seemed to be sounding a bit more cooperative. Rhys relaxed a bit.

Rhys cocked an eyebrow at her. "The sort that deals with plenty of bar fights, drunken brawls, and company barbeques." The thought occurred to him then that this was exactly what had transpired and he actually let out a chuckle. "Wait, wait, wait. You didn't get into a bar fight, did you?" Analise looked a bit sour and averted eye contact by turning her head to the side. Rhys laughed far more easily at this. "Unbelievable. An uptight little city girl like you? Wouldn't have expected that one, Shepherd," he said with a smirk, reapplying the slab of meat in spite of her protests.

"Yeah, well, me neither," she answered dryly. "I was in there looking for dinner. Apparently this town shuts down after 7pm and your bar's the only thing open. Oh, and, apparently, it's totally acceptable to be completely shit faced by 7:30 pm too." "You don't say," Rhys replied, still finding the entire situation far more amusing than he should have. There was something horribly vindicating by Shepherd's black eye. A part of him wanted to clap the omega on the back for a job well done.

"MMm," she answered in a completely irritated tone. She was smirking a lot, as if finding some sort of dry humor in all of this. "Your buddies down the hall decided to bother me and their waitress with some rather rude solicitations followed by inappropriate physical contact. When they crossed the line, I suggested they cease and desist or face criminal charges."

"Bet that worked out for you," Rhys chuckled again. Given who was presently sitting in the drunk tank, he imagined that did not go over really well.

"Oh tremendously. When they refused to see my logic, I had no option but to use force to subdue them while we waited for the local police to not respond to the 911 call and walk their worthless asses fifty feet down the street to assist a fellow officer. So, I had no choice but to bring them here one by one while your impotent staff tried to figure out what to do." Analise pushed the meat away with more determination. "I-I'm sorry. I'm a vegetarian," she explained in a surprisingly personable tone. "And the smell of that is actually churning my stomach right now."

Rhys sat back in his chair which he had pulled across from her to dabble at her swelling face with the rib eye. He offered her a confused frown, though she hardly knew why. For all she knew, he was irritated at how his police force responded. In reality, he was trying to figure out how a woman her size had managed to subdue four male werewolves, one of whom was a gamma.

"What." She essentially demanded through a tired sigh.

"... you really did all that?... Those aren't some piss off city boys; they're country boys who scrap every week. Besides, you look like hell ran you over with a monster truck."

Analise rolled her eyes but did offer an amused grin and chuckle. Analise not trying to run the world was actually somewhat enjoyable. She had a dry sense of humor that Rhys could appreciate, and once her professionalism went down, she could cuss like any drunken cowboy he'd ever met; and fight like one too, apparently. "Yeah, well, you should see the other guys." she let out in an exasperated sigh as she pushed herself up. "Obviously I'm pressing charges. If you'll excuse me, I need to call my lawyer back." She stepped away, pulling out her phone again, though she did cast a hint of a smirk back at Rhys. He was right, a part of her did find this entertaining.

Curiously, Rhys peaked his head down the hallway to see Brody stepping out of the drunk tank with a confused look on his face. "They said she beat 'em up, boss," he replied in his usual flat baritone. Brody shrugged apathetically as he made for the door. "Let 'em sober up and give 'em to me in the morning. If they're scared of a little human girl, then obviously they need some more training. Fucking pussies." "How bad is it?" Rhys inquired, obviously still very curious.

Brody shrugged again. "Lotta missing teeth and bruises. Pretty sure Sam's nose is broken, but he'll live. Said she went all kung Fu on 'em, like I give a damn. Sounds like they got too rowdy and started making some passes at women who weren't interested. When one of 'em wouldn't take no for an answer, your girlfriend told them to back off and, apparently, they announced that they weren't afraid of the FBI and Ric took a swing at her. She knocked out his front teeth with the butt of her pistol and all hell broke loose. They managed to land a few good hits on her, but..." Brody shifted slightly, crossing his arms over his chest.

"Look, Rhys, I don't like where this is heading. Everyone's been talking about her all day. Say she's a werewolf hunter or some shit. Honestly, those four are idiots, but that don't mean a human should stand a chance against them if they're up for a scrap. And a tiny little piss-off human female? It doesn't make sense. Oh and worse, and the omega's have themselves all worked up that she's gonna root out the den or something."

Brody shook his head in dismay. "Don't worry, man. I'll beat enough shit out of them for this one that the others will think twice before fucking up this bad again. I'm more worried about keeping it under control. What's this going to do for morale when they hear that a one-hundred-pound woman beat the shit out of four of our hunters?"

Rhys frowned as his heart sunk in disappointment. His men were better than this. Whatever else she was, Analise was a human woman and those were's had no reason to believe that she'd be able to defend herself. They easily could have killed her. Rhys considered for a moment that that would have made things a lot easier on him. Federal Agent killed in a bar fight? No one would even bat an eye at that sort of thing. At least not in a way that would threaten the pack.

He sighed again. "Yeah, fine," he let out at Brody, who answered with a nod. "She says she's pressing charges. Make sure they all have clean identities for when people start digging," he added, thinking again how close this call had been.

Rhys heard the old pick up roar into life as Brody drove it back to the den. He shook his head as he headed back to the conference room, dismissing most of the night staff, and stopping by the coffee pot and pouring a mug for him and the apparent martial artist. It was day old and luke warm. He smirked at the anticipation of her displeasure over it. It was petty, he knew, but he was still going to enjoy it.

Rhys stepped into the conference room as Analise was hanging up the phone, silently offering her a mug while taking a seat. "Thanks," she replied, taking a sip and contorting her face in disapproval. Rhys could only smirk at the reaction.

"So," Rhys started, taking a sip of his equally horrible brew. "You're a vegetarian, cat loving, kung fu master. Any other character flaws I should know about?" He pulled out a flask from his breast pocket of his jacket and dumped a good amount of clear liquid into his drink, offering some to her as well.

Shepherd hesitated for a moment before shrugging and accepting. "Thanks," she muttered, taking a sip and wincing. "But seriously, are you withholding crime stats? Frankly, I don't care; that's for your district attorney to deal with, not me. I'm just worried about the impact on the case."

Rhys rolled his eyes. "Why yes, Rhys, I'm also obsessed with my work so much that I use it to avoid social contact, now that you ask," he retorted before resting his cobalt blue eyes on hers and shaking his head. "I want to find Allison, Agent Shepherd. Riverton's a close knit community. You think I want to go to church on Sunday and look her pop in the eyes without knowing I've done everything I could to bring his little girl home? Police officer aside, what sort of man does that make me?"

This seemed to be a reasonable explanation as far as Analise was concerned and she both shrugged and nodded her acquiescence at the same time.

Rhys just shook his head at her. "You got any friends, Shepherd? Someone you can call and bitch to about having to defend a waitress's honor against a bunch of drunk lumberjacks?" The statement was light hearted, but hearing what had happened had earned Analise a measure of his respect. Sure, she was rigid and uncompromising, but at least she had her head on straight.

Analise actually chuckled at the Question. "No, not really," she replied. "That would violate the obsession with work as a means of avoiding social contact rule," she added, her eyes twinkling just a bit at the jab. In truth, she kind of found Rhys attractive.

"How about you?" She countered. "Anyone you can call up and complain about the overbearing FBI agent who just stormed in and took over?"

Rhys offered her an amused grin. "Touche, Agent Shepherd, touche." He took another swig of his coffee- other tincture and set the glass down before looking at her again. "How 'bout we try this a little different," he suggested. This was new territory for him and if he was right, it would be for her too.

"I'm listening," she replied with a curiously cocked eyebrow. She casually sipped her coffee-other, watching him over the brim of the mug.

"How about, we try working together instead of trying to beat each other into submission every chance we g et? I'm pretty sure neither of us are going to back down which means we're just getting in each other's way. Not really fair to Allison and those other girls, in my opinion."

Analise was still watching him carefully though she obviously took his suggestion to heart. "Not really my style," she admitted. "But you've got a valid reason." She thought for another second. "Ok, Captain, you've got yourself a deal."

She chuckled slightly and shook her head in confusion. "I'll tell you... I'm pretty sure I'm missing something," she admitted. All the bite of her dominant personality was gone, replaced instead by analytical cooperation.

The honesty of her tone went a long way with Rhys, who, was growing equally tired of butting heads with her every step of the way. This new world of cooperation just might work out after all. "Don't know about that," he answered honestly. "You found their campsite didn't you?"

Analise dismissed the suggestion with a wave. "A transient day camp," she explained as if it weren't of consequence. She was right but Rhys suspected she had no idea why. "They have Allison holed up somewhere and we're running out of time. They won't do anything until they have a full moon. We've only got a week left before that hits and then we'll never find her."

She leaned into the table, making direct eye contact with Rhys. At first he decidedly hated when she did this, but now, he was finding it was actually sort of nice to look someone in the eyes when speaking with them. Her eyes were nice, too. A pretty green with bright grey and brown flexes. Unless you actually looked at them, they just looked green, but now he could see all of the rich complexity in them.

"We need to look at that first area," she revealed, much to Rhys's displeasure. It reminded him that he would either have to kill or turn her; just when things were starting to go his way for a change. "I was looking at a topographical map, and I'm pretty sure there are cave formations in that area. I'm telling you, it's an ideal location for these people. In all my studies, I've not seen something so perfect for them."

Rhys cocked an eyebrow and shrugged. And here he looked on his den location with disdain. The werewolf hunter's description almost made him blush with pride. "I suppose we can go take a look at it in the morning," he suggested, already regretting that it would likely result in him having to put the woman down.

"But-" Analise started to argue.

"Absolutely not," he interrupted impatiently. "No way in hell I'm dragging you out into the woods at this time of night when you just got the snot knocked out of you."

Shepherd's brow ruffled in offense. "I'm perfectly fine," she insisted. "Just a few bruises. Not even noteworthy." "Noteworthy enough for you to press charges," he returned. "It can wait for morning when we've got some better light. Here," he said, retrieving her glass and standing up. "I'll walk you back to your hotel. I'll get you first thing in the morning and we'll see if your cult spotting is just luck or if you've actually got a talent in it," he promised.

"Fine," she answered begrudgingly as she stood up to join him at the door.

They both paused at the threshold at the same time. The precinct was deathly quiet and Analise frowned from the eerie familiarity. Rhys was frowning for a much more concerning reason. He smelled the rogue alpha and at least five other were's with him. "Something's not right," Analise muttered as she reached for her Glock.

"Get back in the conference room and stay low," Rhys ordered in full on General Rhys voice. Oddly, Analise seemed to approve of the tone, though she had no intention of obeying him. Some sixth sense of hers was telling her what Rhys's nose had confirmed: Danger was clear and present.

Rhys carefully stepped out into the main room of the precinct. He smelled fresh blood and looked cautiously to note that the nightshift secretary was laying perfectly still on the floor behind the reception desk in a pool of dark red.

The man steeled himself against the visage, rage boiling up inside. He knew what was going on. It would be impossible to cover it up now. As soon as he killed this alpha, he'd start evacuating the pack. Maybe a neighboring pack would take them in as refugees or something. Rhys wasn't optimistic.

He could still smell the alpha and knew he was still in the building somewhere. The scent of the other wolves wafted to him as well. They had mostly shifted into their wolf forms, which was going to make this even harder.

A small sound from behind indicated that Agent Shepherd had spotted the body of the secretary. It was only then that Rhys was relieved to have her around.

Any other woman would have gasped, maybe cried out, and most likely would have backed away in terror upon seeing that much blood around a lifeless body. Any other woman would be a liability in this moment, and Rhys wouldn't have thought less of her for it. It took a special person to stomach that much gore without mentally breaking down. He was one such person. Apparently, so was Shepherd.

For all the head butting, all the battles for dominance and control, Shepherd was no different than he was. She was a human version of an Alpha female just looking out for her own family and people as best she could. It was in that moment that Rhys realized he understood her better than he had thought. All of her stand-offish behavior, all of her arrogance and "all-business" mannerisms, they were all a defense mechanism to help her deal with the pressures of being an Alpha in a world that needed them, but certainly didn't understand them.

Rhys didn't have time to ponder these implications. The Alpha wolf was too much of a threat and had already killed out in the open. Rhys gestured for

Shepherd to move to his right and cover him as he stepped forward to check the secretary for a pulse. Shepherd nodded once and veered right without question, eying the room carefully for any sign of trouble as she went.

Thank god, Rhys thought in relief as the difficult woman worked perfectly with him, rather than taking this as a chance to assert that she was in charge. It was one less thing to have to worry about and he actually felt a measure of comfort knowing that a perfectionist like her had his back.

Rhys padded over to the lifeless body with the skill of the silent predator that lived inside of him. Carefully, he stooped and delicately pressed his hand to what remained of the woman's neck. He wasn't even sure why he was checking for a pulse; there was no way she had survived the attack. The cold stillness at his fingertips confirmed it and also solidified his resolve. This alpha was as good as dead.

The snapping sound from behind the receptionist desk instantly drew his attention and he jerked his to the side with just enough time to see the enormous wolf jump out and tackle him. Rhys's hands went up instinctively to shield his face and neck from the maw of teeth violently snapping for him. Given the size, this was likely a beta, not that it was going to help Rhys's odds in human form.

The beast wrestled with Rhys for control, ripping and tearing at the meat of his arm, and just when Rhys considered shifting to finish this fight quickly, two gun shots echoed through the precinct and the large beta was hurled to Rhys's left, dropping dead before it hit the ground. Rhys had just enough time to whip his head to the right and take in Shepherd, still in her kneeling firing position with the barrel of her Glock still aimed at his direction and smoking.

"Rhys! Look out!" She shouted, jumping to her feet just as the Alpha male came barreling out of a dark hall way, heading straight for Shepherd. The male was followed by three other betas, all in wolf form, and quickly descending upon the duo faster than they could respond.

Shepherd emptied the rest of her clip at the alpha male with little result. She had landed two bullets in its shoulder, but a head shot was the only thing that would bring a wolf like that down. The beast snarled and growled as it lunged forward, leaving Shepherd little option but to bolt down the hall and out of the building entirely.

Rhys panicked and shifted in an instant. The 260 lb. wolf shred through his clothing like tissue paper and tackled the first beta that dared to attack him. As far as alphas went, Rhys was somewhere in the middle. The rogues' alpha was slightly larger than he was, but these betas were no match for the black and grey haired wolf with deep blue eyes, even with his injured arm.

Rhys veritably roared as he pounced on an approaching enemy, pinning him to the ground and tearing out his throat in a gory display of violence and dominance. Another beta took the opportunity to attack him from behind, essentially mounting him and clamping his teeth into the back of Rhys's neck.

The powerful alpha was nothing but rage and hardly even felt as the razor sharp teeth sunk deeply into his skin. With a violent shake, he sent the beta soaring into a nearby wall, the tell-tale sounds of cracking ribs echoing through the building. The beta yelped in pain at the hit but remained undaunted in his approach. He stumbled to try and regain his footing just as Rhys was upon him.

Rhys's maw found the tender and exposed neck with a seasoned ease and dug his razor sharp claws into the beta's soft belly. In a single move, he both ripped and tore at the smaller wolf, freeing his trachea and spilling his guts all over the tile floor at once.

At this point, the final beta decided to fall back. He was trying to back away from Rhys and follow after the alpha, but Rhys had lost complete control over his ability to think rationally and was driven only by the need to spill their blood. They all had to die and it was going to be horrific.

The powerful alpha lunged at the beta and latched onto its hind leg. The beta let out a yelp of panic, howling for his alpha to come aid him, but it was fruitless. In a violent shake, Rhys yanked the leg out of socket, causing the beta to wail in pain. In another shake, he had almost completely torn the leg off.

Desperately, the beta wolf struggled to bite at Rhys's face and neck, but his wound was terrible and he was already starting to bleed out. Rhys batted away the useless efforts and sunk his teeth into the beta's throat, again ripping it free and ending the pitiful creature's suffering once and for all.

Rage still filled the alpha's cobalt blue eyes and he didn't even pause as he took off into the night after the alpha who dared to chase after a female in his domain...

********* Analise ran as fast she could into the darkness of the night. She knew she wouldn't be a match for the wolf's speed and it was closing in on her. Her only solution, not a terribly good one, was to weave around and take sharp turns. It would be harder for the animal to get it's speed up without straight distances.

The woman was panting uncontrollably as she sped past the forest tree line and into the uneven terrain of the woods ahead. Maybe I could climb a tree or something? She thought in uncertainty as she whipped around a boulder and slid down a steep embankment.

The wolf had more trouble with the embankment and it bought her some time. Analise reached for another magazine, only to discover that she didn't have one on her. She had emptied all of her bullets at this thing already anyway with disappointing results. Worse, Analise was sure this was some trained wolf belonging to the cult. A normal wolf would have given up already. Hell, a normal wolf wouldn't have wandered into the police precinct loaded with smells and sounds of people.

The wolf began to close the distance between them just as Analise saw a slender tree in view. In a sprinting dash, she jumped for the tree and used her momentum to swing around, planting both heels into the wolf's chest. The beast was kicked backward, yelping in the shocking pain that it most certainly wasn't expecting, as Analise took off again.

Off in the distance, Analise thought she could make out the forms of campers around a fire. Tents, the smell of stew, everything about them spoke to being campers. "HEY!" Analise screamed as she ran, her voice cracking from the fatigue that was already settling in. "HEY! There's a wolf! HELP!" She let out.

If she was lucky, and she never was, one of them would have a gun. At the very least, it would be a fight between five people and one wolf instead of one person and one wolf.

Analise bolted toward the camp as fast as she could. The people were standing up and looking at her curiously and it was only as she approached that she realized in horror who they were. This damn wolf had driven her directly into the hands of the cultists!

Her eyes widened and panic began setting in. She was out of ammo and out of breath to continue running like this. If the wolf didn't finish her off, these people would be able to catch her without even trying. Analise tried to slow down and then thought to change directions suddenly, which only resulted in her toppling painfully to the ground. By that point, one of the men had already run over to her and yanked her up by the arm.

Analise looked wildly behind her. The enormous wolf was now replaced with a man who was even bigger than Rhys, and, who was naked from head to toe.

"Heh, look what I found, Marek," the man holding her arm offered with an almost sinister chuckle.

Analise frowned and slammed the hilt of her glock into the guy's face, flipping the gun in the air and pistol whipping him a second time across the temple. She felt as the cartilage of his nose gave way, flattening it to his face. Instantly, the man released her and cupped his injuries while howling in pain.

Analise tried to dash away, only to be grabbed roughly by the large naked guy, presumably named Marek, and thrown heavily to the ground. The others stood around and watched, entertained in some sort of sick pleasure as Marek roughly handled the smaller woman.

Analise knew she wasn't going to win this one, but she wasn't going down without a fight. As Marek advanced on her, she shot a foot upward, connecting solidly with his partial erection. Marek looked like he was going to be sick for a moment, and then just channeled the pain into anger. Analise was scrambling to regain her footing, only to have Marek roughly grab at her legs and yank her toward him.

She continued to fight, thrusting the heel of her hand upward into his face, only to have him grab her wrist and flip around to her stomach, painfully twisting her arm behind her back and pinning her to the ground. He tangled his fingers into her hair and jerked her head upward, causing her to strain just to breath and keep her shoulder in its socket.

Marek snarled at her in fury, blood dripping from the bullet wounds that grazed his arm and shoulder. "Fucking bitch," he hissed, wanting nothing more than to finish her right there. "Bitch fucking shot me and broke my ribs," he complained, tightening his hold on her arm until she let out a cry of pain.

One of the men who watched rolled his eyes. "Poor Marek got his ass kicked by a puny little human girl," the man mocked in humor.

"You shut the fuck up," Marek barked at the man before returning his gaze to the squirm woman beneath his grip. "Got her, didn't I? Besides... she's an alpha female." Marek let out a wicked laugh of victory. "Oh you'll make a fine little bitch for someone, I'm sure," he hackled at her as he added enough pressure to her arm to cause her to cry out again in pain. "And you smell delicious too," he added in a heady voice.

Analise's heart sank into her stomach. Killing her was what she had expected. Raping her? She wasn't mentally prepared for the assault and doubled her squirming to try and wriggle free of Marek's iron tight hold.

Marek merely smirked at her efforts. He wasn't too worried about breaking her and had no worries about taking her roughly. From what he had observed, she handled herself just fine against those stupid omegas in the bar. After he had turned her, he would claim her as his mate, which would put him in an excellent standing among the others. The first high alpha female in almost a century? Marek would be sitting on a lot of power with that one.

Still, he had to beat her down first. He had no intention of turning her right away, if he could help it. No, he'd have a little fun with his prize first, at least until he could control her.

Analise let out something akin to a battle cry as she bucked her hips in an attempt to throw him off of her. Marek smiled again. "Oh that's what you want? You are a feisty little bitch, aren't you?"

"Get the fuck off of me, you psychopath!" She hissed violently, grabbing a handful of dirt with her free hand and tossing it to where she hoped was his face.

Marek sneezed a bit and gripped her even harder, clearly irritated by the move. "What do you say, boys? Should I give his little bitch what she wants? Can't seem to wait for it, can you, honey?"

The surrounding men let out chuckles of approval, reclining back to watch the scene unfold as if they were impassively watching a good porno. Analise had not stopped resisting. She knew, somewhere in her mind, that it was only going to hurt worse this way, but the defiant spark that had come to define her preferred it that way. She wasn't going to confuse consensual rough sex with rape. The more it hurt, the easier it would be to do so.

In a deft move, Marek had begun ripping open her jeans. He would release his grip on her only knowing that she would try to get up, so that he could better position her for tearing off more of her clothes.

Analise gasped as the cold night air assaulted her bare skin. Marek flopped her over to her back, grasping tightly around her throat has he kept her pinned to the forest floor. He had already start to grab at her hoodie and tee-shirt, ripping or yanking to expose as much of her skin as possible until she was left with an open hoodie, her bra, and her already torn panties.

Analise choked at his hold, gasping painfully for air and clawing alternately at his hand or his face. Marek was neither deterred nor impressed and he moved himself over her, forcing her legs apart as he pressed the tip of his hard cock into her unprepared flesh.

"Don't worry, little bitch," he mocked her. "I'll have you moaning before I'm through with you." Marek eyed her neck and his eyes seemed to fill with lust and power. Somehow he knew he wouldn't be able to hold back. The way she fought him, her scent... Marek could barely restrain from shifting. There was no way he'd not bite her.

Marek shrugged a bit. He didn't really care. The little woman was worth a lot of respect as far as the council was concerned and he was pretty sure a lot of those old farts would pay well to get a chance to fuck her. He'd have the first taste, though. Owning a bitch like her? Marek could have a lot more influence in the larger politics of Lycanthropes worldwide.

With that, Marek thrust his dick forward, eliciting a horrified and garbled scream from the woman beneath him. She was deliciously tight and the friction of her dry pussy against his cock seemed to arouse him further. He didn't care how much he hurt her; she was supposed to be some sort of alpha female, after all. She could take it and would take it as often as he wanted it. He started pumping in and out, only concerned with his own delight, as he dipped his head down and harshly sank his teeth into her neck.

Shepherd closed her eyes briefly, never stopping in her fight, and it was in that brief moment that she felt Marek yanked off of her. Analise's eyes popped open and she pushed herself up, scuttling away until her back hit a tree. She grasped at the bleeding wound on her neck and watched the unfolding gore with wide eyes.

An enormous black and grey wolf had charged the camp, leading behind him almost twenty other huge wolves of various sizes and colors. The men who had been sitting by idly now jumped to their feet and to Analise's horror, they shifted from men into similarly sized wolves, joining in the battle.

She almost didn't believe her eyes. They... they turned into wolves? Her eyes found Marek, who was engaged in a fight with the giant black and grey wolf. She watched without blinking as the beast of a man shifted into the large red wolf that had attacked the precinct. Marek was the same wolf who had chased her down. The comment about being shot and struck in the ribs suddenly made a lot more sense.

Both of the larger two wolves fought viciously, as if they had everything to lose. Each wrestled for dominance, spinning and flipping, gnawing and snapping. There was blood splattering everywhere. The black and grey wolf had a horrible injury to his right leg, Analise observed, but he was doing his best to ignore it in his seemingly epic battle with the wolf man who had just assaulted her. And epic it certainly was. Regardless of who won, the victor would be in tough shape afterward.

The rest of the wolves seemed to make easy enough work of the remaining men, largely because of strength in number. The fight was working in the favor of the attackers and Analise found herself rooting for them. If she had to guess, they weren't as strong of fighters as the ones they were attacking, but all the same, anything taking out these people was putting her mind at some sort of ease.

The world was starting to close off to her. She suddenly became very aware of her breathing; it and the thumping of her heart were the only sounds she could hear. Everything felt like it was moving in slow motion and nothing she saw made any sense at all. Her eyes drifted to the edge of the fire light. A woman was standing there, watching Analise with impassive interest. Her green eyes seemed to flicker in the firelight. She was... familiar

"... Laura?" Analise found herself whispering, not even fully believing herself. It was too much information for her injured form to handle and Analise's eyes rolled back in her head as she slumped over, passed out. Analise awoke with a start. "Laura!" She let out in a gasping breath. She blinked her eyes a few times to adjust to the synthetic white of fluorescent bulbs. The jerking movement quickly proved itself as her entire body seared in pain. Between the bar fight, the marathon run, and the starting of getting raped, Agent Shepherd's body finally gave out and she had no choice but to succumb to the pain.

The woman let out a moan as she eased back down into what she assumed was a hospital bed. The room certainly looked that way, though there weren't any windows in her room to distinguish whether or not she was still in Riverton or some other city.

Analise wearily examined her arms, about the only thing she could lift without hurling herself further into exhaustion. They were covered with bruises and scrapes and littered with the occasional stitch. Rhys hadn't been kidding; she really did look like hell ran her over with a monster truck.

The thought caused her to smirk slightly until she remembered what had happened to him. Rhys was likely dead, mauled to death by the cult's wolves. Analise's expression sunk into misery. She had tried to save him, hadn't she? Sure she thought. Just like I tried to save Laura.

Memories of that night almost thirty years ago started to play out in her mind...

Laura had snuck out in the woods to meet her boyfriend. She was obviously sick of her irritating little sister following her around, but Analise had snuck out and followed after her anyway.

Analise walked through the woods with nothing but the moonlight and her My Little Ponies flashlight to guide her. She had been thankful, unconsciously so, for the full moon. Her little flashlight was really more of a novelty than anything useful. Still, the five-year-old girl wandered after her older sister, clutching to her cabbage patch kid for support as she wound her way along the path.

Analise could hear Laura giggling and whispering off in the distance, some unknown teenaged boy replying with giggles and whispers of his own. As the little child rounded the corner, intent on jumping out to surprise her sister, she heard Laura let out a frightened scream. Everything had happened so quickly. Laura was screaming and the teenaged boy was shouting. In a few seconds, a fight had broken out between the boy and a large man Analise had never seen before.

The terrified child crouched behind a bush, too afraid to move or run for help. The stranger snapped the teenaged boy's neck in a sickening crack, letting the lifeless body fall haphazardly to the ground as he menacingly stared down Laura. Laura's eyes were as wide as quarters. She tried to turn and run, but the stranger grabbed her by the hair and yanked her backward.

Analise hadn't known what to do, but bravery and courage suddenly started to swell inside of her. Mustering every ounce of it she had, the little girl jumped from the bush and began punching and kicking the man holding onto her sister. For all her best efforts, the man simply offered her a callous laugh, kicking her easily aside.

"Don't worry, little pup," he had told her in disregard. "You'll have your day soon enough." Another kick to Analise's stomach was enough to keep her down. The man tossed the screaming Laura over his shoulder and disappeared into the night without a trace.

Present day Analise frowned as the memory flashed before her. She had tried and failed to save her sister which was no better than doing nothing at all. Everything she had become was so that she would never fail again and here she lay in this hospital while Rhys was probably dead and Allison Reed and the other missing girls were probably still just that: missing.

Analise let out a dismal sigh as she rolled her head to the side. She was surprised to see an old woman sitting in a chair not too far from her bed, giving Analise another jolting start. The old woman's eyes had been watching Analise the whole time, appearing both ancient and eerie to the younger woman.

"D... do I know you?" Analise asked innocently. Her tone was about as far from General Shepherd as it could be. In reality, she just sounded like a heart broken, sweet woman.

"No," Came the woman's reply. "But I attend to you none-the-less."

Analise's brow flickered lightly in confusion but she tried not to appear ungrateful. "Th-thank you.... Where am I? Who are you?"

"You are in our center for healing," the old woman replied. "I am Isa. You are Analise Shepherd."

Confusion started to tickle at Analise. She was too tired to even push herself up and she could barely keep her eyes open. "I... yep, that's me," she answered, clearly unsure of herself. "Captain Forrester? Is he ok? A wolf bit him...." Analise slowly started to realize that she had work to do and awkwardly pushed at the blankets. "I've... I've got to find the girls," she offered weakly. "What day is it?"

Isa hushed her with a gentle tone. "You are in no condition for this," she replied. "The girl child, Allison, was found. She is with her parents. The other girls were taken to their homes and are with their parents. Your efforts were instrumental in this."

Relief flooded through Analise and she stopped struggling to get up for the moment. "Good... That's good..." This was not the Analise that had been described to Isa. She had only heard stories about the brutally harsh, arrogant FBI agent who had stirred up so much fear and tension with her keen ability to locate were's. No, this was a woman who obviously cared for the well-being of others and who threw all of her potential into trying to protect them. The harshness was just a manifestation of what she really was; an alpha female. "What about Rhys?" She asked in the same caring and fragile voice. This one was laced with uncertainty.

"He is badly injured," Isa reported. "Who is Laura?"

Analise sank visibly. It was her fault. She shouldn't have missed when she was shooting at the huge wolf. It was all her fault. "Can... can I see him?" She asked as guilt permeated into her tone.

"No," Isa replied bluntly. "He is badly injured."

Agent Shepherd brought a weak hand up to her head, resting it across her eyes. "Fine," she let out, clearly disappointed. "Any idea when he'll be well enough for visitors?"

"I do not know," Isa answered cryptically, implying a dual meaning. "I will give him a message if you wish."

Analise perked up slightly, looking over to the woman with curiosity and hope. "Can... can you tell him I'm sorry?"

Isa returned the curious look. "Why are you sorry?" She wondered out loud.

Some internal hurt began to surface. "... he's hurt because of me," she said simply. "Because I messed up. I got him involved in something way over his head and he only did it because he was worried about his community. I'm just... I really am sorry."

Isa's curiosity was still getting the better of her. "If you were in his position, and you felt your kin was in danger, would you have acted differently?"

Analise snorted slightly. "You mean if I thought a cult was moving into the forest around my home town? Yeah, I'd burn down the forest and slaughter every one of those sick bastards who made it out alive." She shrugged slightly, wincing in the pain she felt where her left shoulder and neck met. That asshole Marek had bit her pretty hard. "Seriously though, baring that sort of unrealism, no. I would probably have responded like him and do what I could to help out the cocky FBI agent who showed claiming to have all the answers."

Isa lifted her eyebrows at Analise's drastic solution to a threat to her pack. That was the sort of dedication that the alphas of old had toward their own; it was something that was lost in this era with all the panic over the females dying.

Meanwhile, Agent Shepherd haphazardly pawed at the bandaging along her neck. She had been raped, she realized. She still felt emotionally numb over the issue. Had the cult done that to Laura too? She pressed her eyes closed and a tear spilled out from underneath.

Without the missing girls or Rhys to worry about all of the emotional turmoil from the event began to surface.

"Can I use a phone?" Analise asked pitifully. "I need to start filing my report... "

"No," Isa said bluntly as she stood from her chair. "You must rest. The phone will be there when you are stronger."

Analise wanted to argue, but she couldn't even get out of the bed. She had almost no dexterity in her fingers, so even they would let her use a laptop, it would take her an hour just to type a paragraph. As the older woman left the room, Analise's heavy eyes pulled shut, lulling her into the horrors of post-traumatic stress induced nightmares...

Rhys was pacing back and forth in his room. They had bandaged up his arm well enough, but even with his super werewolf healing rates, they estimated it would take several months to fully heal after that beta had shredded so much of the muscle. That he didn't have full use of his arm and had to wear this stupid sling was only furthering his anxious and irritable state.

Brody was sitting in a wheel chair opposite him, looking irritated himself. His leg was propped up and a sort of cast filled with pins surrounded it. The battle had been the worst in pack history and everyone had the scars to prove it.

Rhys's pacing only stopped when Isa made her way in, calmly approaching a chair and taking a seat. Rhys's face lit up with worry reborn. "How is she? Is she awake? Did she say anything?"

Isa lifted an eyebrow at the speed and insistence at which the questions came. "She awoke briefly. The change is happening very quickly and taking much of her energy. Her blood is well suited for our kind. She will make a strong wolf."

Rhys fell heavily into a chair and buried his face in his remaining good hand. "This is all my fault," he growled miserably.

"Interestingly, she believes the same," Isa replied.

Rhys rolled his eyes. He had witnessed Analise single handedly dispatch a Beta and then, after sprinting a full mile, kick an Alpha with enough force to break his ribs. That would have been difficult for any female in wolf form and should have been impossible for a human, regardless of gender. She did so much more than what was expected that Rhys thought she deserved a medal of valor.

"That's stupid," Rhys retorted. "What could she have done about this? Hell, she was the one who figured out how to find them to begin with. It was my responsibility and I failed. Simple as that."

CHAPTER 3

Isa growled at Rhys, challenging his dominance in a very rare display of her own. "Then you are stupid too. She is human and thinks as humans think. She could not have known the full scope of the danger, but in her eyes, she held all of the knowledge and improperly gave it to you. Did you not agree to work together?" Isa challenged. "To cooperate? To do so is to share in responsibility. You are both to blame. You are both the hero, and in your eyes, Rhys Forester, you are both stupid."

The hair on the back of Rhys's neck stood as the irrational wolf within considered attacking Isa. Brody offered a skeptical and mildly concerned look before turning to Isa with a question. "Did she say anything about Laura?"

Laura, they learned, was a dominant female in the rogue pack. She was also Analise's sister, though the Agent believed her to be dead. The dynamic intrigued Brody more than anyone else and he had expended a great deal of energy trying to learn more about the situation.

Isa shook her head. "She was preoccupied with the condition of Rhys and the safety of the four human women. She also wishes to contact her superiors and begin reporting on this situation. I have delayed her, but this will not resolve the issue. Once her strength returns, it will be difficult to achieve her compliance."

Rhys frowned. "I'm going to go talk to her," he said with resolution.

"No," Isa barked. "You must let her rest."

Rhys growled again and stepped menacingly toward the old woman. "Damn it, Isa, I've had about enough out of you," he snapped furiously. "I've finally got the pack convinced that our little werewolf hunter just acted on our behalf, you're sitting here implying that as soon as she comes to, it's back to being our enemy again, and now you're telling me not to fix this? Don't talk to me like I'm some stupid pup who can't figure this shit out!"

Isa growled again and Brody half expected them to throw down right there. No one, Rhys included, ever spoke to Isa the way he just had. "Uh... maybe I should leave..." Brody suggested hesitantly.

"Your hormones are affecting your judgment," Isa returned dangerously. "Her scent has affected you."

Rhys looked like he was about to blow a gasket as his face turned cherry red with anger. "If you ever, ever make that suggestion again, I'll rip out your throat, you hear me?" He answered in a gravelly voice.

Isa did not back down. "It is affecting me as well," she continued, much to Rhys and Brody's surprise. "She is a High Alpha. The chaos which is to ensue has only just begun."

"What's a High Alpha?" Rhys asked skeptically.

"The wolves on the council are High Alphas," Isa replied. "Analise is the first female High Alpha in almost two hundred years. They are as fierce and ruthless as any alpha male but far more dangerous. As her turning completes, Analise will produce a pheromone that will enable her to control the weak and influence the strong. Even now it has begun. You desire to protect your pack from her but you would choose diplomacy over the correct action."

"I'm not going to kill her," he snapped.

"In your position, she would," replied Isa. "I asked her how she would solve this problem; a strong pack hiding in the woods, threatening her own pack. Your solution was to search the woods and kill them. It was the solution expected of an Alpha Male. Hers? She would set the woods ablaze. An Alpha shows little mercy or restraint when dealing with his enemies. A High Alpha shows none. There is a reason that those men compose the council. They are feared by all because they act with finality. Their dedication to their packs is absolute and without question."

"And she hates werewolves and wants to kill us all," said Brody through a sardonic sigh. "Great. Your girlfriend's turning out to be a real charmer, Rhys," he added through a snort.

"Brody, so help me," Rhys warned in a dangerously trembling voice. He turned to Isa with a hard glare. "I can convince her that we aren't a threat," he said surely. "I understand her. I think I even have her respect a little and if you're serious that she's concerned about my wellbeing, then that only works in our favor."

"The problem is broader than this," Isa said, not disagreeing with his intent. "The Council Males have all lost their mates to this disease. The High Alphas were the first to perish. They will all desire her as a mate. There will be war."

Rhys blinked a few times at this. Some part of his mind was already considering the idea of courting the woman. She had all of the characteristics he was searching for in a mate. He assumed there would be battles with other packs, other alphas trying to claim her for their own, but having to fight off the council? There was no way. Their pack barely fended off a group of rogues. If the Council sent in even a small pack of their best alphas, the Forester pack would be decimated.

The disappointment Rhys suddenly felt was obvious to everyone. "Ok, then I really need to talk to her," he said in an accepting voice.

Isa frowned. "Did you not hear my words?" She countered sharply.

"Yeah," he interrupted before she could lecture him some more. "I heard you. You said that she's going to be some Council level wolf. If we're about to get into a battle with the Council, then she's the one running the show, not any of us," he said frankly. "And Brody's right; she hates wolves. Regardless of what she ends up being, my responsibility is to protect this pack and as it stands, she's the worst threat we've ever seen. I've got to eliminate that threat and if that means making her our ally, then that's what I'm going to do. That's the only way we come out of this in one piece." Rhys didn't wait for a response as he quietly and calmly left the room.

Brody and Isa sat in stunned silence for a moment. "You know," Brody approached curiously, "If that's the effect these pheromones of her has on him, I think it's an improvement."

Isa nodded sagely. "Rhys has begun the path of wisdom," she commented with a sense of pride. "Our pack will soon see the golden age of old and it will be he who leads us there... "

Rhys lost track of how long he had been sitting by her bed. It was long enough for guilt to wash over him and plenty of time for him to feel completely sorry for himself that he wouldn't be able to court her. He wasn't even sure why it bothered him so much. She probably wouldn't have been receptive to begin with and if courting her meant exposing his pack to open war with the Council? How could he be so selfish? Really, it was more the fact that it was no longer possible that bothered him so much. Like a child being told no, now all he could think about was precisely what he couldn't have.

Fortunately, every time he looked at her, guilt completely overwhelmed his senses. She was covered in bruises and deep cuts. The bite on her shoulder looked incredibly painful. Rhys had never bitten a mate, but he knew that he wouldn't have bitten her as hard as that bastard Marek had. It gave him a great sense of pride to know he was the one who ripped out Marek's throat. Even with his shredded arm, it had been Rhys who ran Analise out of the woods, carrying her in his arms. The woman was arrogant, there was no doubt about it, but for whatever reason he had connected with her and felt responsible for her.

She stirred slightly, quietly battling her unseen foe in her nightmares. He thought about waking her up, saving her from the bad dream, but then decided that she needed the rest more than she needed a savior. Eventually, some long while later, her green eyes weakly opened. She had broken out in a sweat as the virus took hold. In a day or so the transformation would be over. The worst of it was still to come.

"... Rhys?" She let out in weak surprise. It caught his attention.

"Analise... you're awake..." he turned to give her his full attention, eyes wide and attentive. "Are you ok? How do you feel?"

She smiled slightly. "You didn't happen to catch the license plate of that monster truck did you?"

Rhys pursed his lips in humor.

"What happened?" She asked. "No one has told me anything and they won't let me use a phone... And where the hell are we?" Analise had decided this whole "healing center" business was a load of bull.

Rhys swallowed slightly and looked away. "I'd tell you, Shepherd, but you aren't going to like it."

Analise's face wrinkled with concern, followed by the flash of understanding. "... I'm infected..." she didn't want to believe it was true, but of course it was. All of her research indicated that the cult members would bite their victims to transmit their virus. So little was known about it, aside from the fact Analise was about to start hallucinating that she could turn into an animal.

Rhys nodded. "Yep. You sure are," he said in a dark sort of dryness.

Analise let out a long and patient sigh. "God damn it." She stared at the ceiling for a moment hoping that this was just some sort of bad dream and she was about to wake up. That didn't happen. "Where am I," she asked again, though more flatly.

"Some place that knows how to handle the sort of disease you just picked up," he answered cryptically.

Analise flashed a disapproving frown. "No offense, Rhys," she told him in standard Agent-Shepherd-is-in- charge tone, "but I think I'd know if such a place actually existed."

"No offense, Analise," he replied sharply, "but I don't think you know what the hell you're talking about." So it was back to beating each other into submission. Great. Just great.

Rhys was deathly silent and kept his eyes locked firmly on hers. Her face hardened as she figured it out. Rhys was infected too. Had it been a set up? It didn't feel that way but... "I'm such a moron... " She whispered to herself, bringing a hand up to massage the bridge of her nose. "... I don't suppose me demanding to be let go is going to do any good, is it?"

"I'm not holding you here against your will," He answered confidently. "Though," he added with a shrug of consideration, "I wouldn't turn down the chance to hear you beg and plead anyway." That didn't elicit the chuckle he had been hoping for. This was going to be harder than he thought. "Sorry," he let out slightly.

He kept his eyes locked firmly on hers as he shifted approaches. "Let me tell you a story, Analise," he said finally. "You can choose whether or not you want to believe me, but I think you're smart enough to tell when you're being lied to or not. You think you know so much about this cult of yours, and frankly for an outsider your knowledge is frighteningly impressive, but... well, you've got a lot of it wrong. If you're willing... well, I am in a uni Hue position to correct some of that for you." Rhys paused to look at her.

"Uni Hue position." She stated as firmly as she could. Her voice was so weak it was hard to hear any bite in it, forced or otherwise. She paused for a while. "You know me, Rhys. At least, well enough to know what I'm going to do the second I get out. You're willing to risk this?"

Rhys gave her a firm sort of look someone offered an adversary. "I think if you hear the truth of it... well there's no doubt about what you'd do if me or mine were anything like those men that attacked you," he said finally. "But we aren't like that. And I don't think you're so heartless that you'd knowingly destroy the lives of so many innocent people."

"See, this cult of yours didn't start thirty years ago. It's a lot older than that. Isa could probably give you the exact date; frankly I don't give a damn. Sometime in the early middle ages, people like me started banding together for protection."

Analise cocked an eyebrow. "From what?" "From people like you," he answered surely. "For right or for wrong, we were being hunted for something we had absolutely no control over. To this day, a lot of us still see it as a curse. Only with modern medicine were they able to determine that it's a virus or parasitic hormone or something. I didn't do too well in biology; someone else could probably explain it better. The point is, we were scared. A bunch of real smart and real deadly people were trying to kill us. If that were you, what would you do?"

"I wouldn't play the empathy card right now if I were you," Analise warned. She already saw where this was going and if she had more energy, she'd have been out of the bed in a heartbeat.

"Fair enough," He said, holding up his good hand in retreat. "But I think you and I have a lot more in common than you realize. I just ask you to keep an open mind is all." "I'm listening," she replied through a tensed jaw. She wasn't happy, but she was trying to hear him out. It was a start.

"Good. Well... these people like me formed groups. We were safer in numbers and we mostly kept to ourselves, living out in the woods where the particulars of our condition wouldn't be so obvious. Advances in the rest of society made it easier in some ways and harder in others. It's pretty hard to explain not having a social security number when you were born long before that even became an idea." Rhys licked his lips nervously, trying to keep himself steady. Analise was beyond pissed and he knew he was testing her patience.

"I'm a hundred and six years old, Shepherd," he told her in complete honesty. "I know you probably don't believe that, but its true none-the-less. About a hundred years ago, this special disease of ours caught a disease of its own. The women started dying. The first to go were the strong ones like you. Left us without female leaders and folks sort of forgot what that meant. They were all dead by the time I came of age and the problem didn't get much better with time. The women who were left stopped having female pups-er, babies. By about thirty years ago, almost ninety percent of our... sub race, for a lack of a better word for it, was male. That's when the Council made their decision."

Analise nodded to indicate that she followed, but her tight jaw told Rhys that her anger had not subsided. "The decision that you, assholes were going to kidnap helpless girls and rape their fucking brains out until they gave you cute little babies girls for you to raise up and do the same? You make me sick, trying to justify this shit to me... "

Rhys gave her a sour look. "You know, I feel the same way about it as you do," he told her seriously, which came as a slight surprise to her. "I'm a bit surprised you'd have thought I would have been onboard with to, Shepherd," he added with a bit of hurt in his voice. "But it is sick; no argument there. That's why me and mine didn't comply with the decree. Came at a high risk too, not following the rules. Following the rules is sort of something our kind does." Rhys shifted slightly in his chair.

"My pack is a family. I know you just see it as some cult that brainwashes people, and maybe some packs are, but we're far from it. Prior to the decree, we would never bring a human in unless there was a good reason and a consensus for it. Even after the decree, nobody is here by force. Nobody was kidnapped or coerced. If I even caught wind of something like that, I'd have slit the offender's throat personally. Now, you can choose not to believe me all you want but that's the god's honest truth. This is a family and family isn't built on lies and abuse."

"What happened to your sister was horrible," he told her finally, meeting her squarely in the eyes. "I've done everything in my power to prevent that from happening here." He paused, looking as deeply into her eyes as he could. "We aren't all like that, Analise. Some of us, like my pack, well... well we aren't that different from you, far as our principles go. I know if anyone even touched one of my kin like what happened to your sister, I'd stop at nothing until that bastard was dead."

Analise turned and looked up at the ceiling, her fists white as she clenched onto the sheets of the bed. "You going to let me go now?" She asked forcefully.

Rhys frowned slightly. He had been hoping for more of a dialogue than this, though in reality he wasn't fully sure what to expect. "Your body is accepting and integrating the virus. You're going to be one of us by the end of the week. 'At's why you've got a fever and feel like shit, I figure."

Analise flinched slightly at hearing the news. It was probably akin to a death knell to her, given her life's work. "And then what?" She asked, the fierceness and harshness of her tone back in full force.

Rhys let out a sigh. "That's up to you," he told her honestly. "You're welcome to stay here, and frankly I think you should for a little while, until after you get a hold of what's happening to you, but like I said, I won't keep you here against your will." He studied her for a moment before continuing. She wasn't carrying on like some child. No, her reaction was far more dangerous.

She absorbed all of the information and seemed to be plotting Rhys's death.

Against his better judgment, he decided to show her one of his cards. "Isa thinks I should kill you. She says you won't show us any mercy and that you won't see the difference between my pack and the others that treated you so badly; you're a threat to us, she thinks."

"I'd say Isa's right," Analise answered sharply. "If I were you, I would have killed me already and not wasted the breath." Analise turned to eye Rhys with heavy criticism. "Fortunately for me, you aren't me." It was as if she were silently calling him a pussy while thanking him at the same time.

That was not the answer Rhys was hoping to hear. He felt a little concerned for the moment, but hid it well enough. "Are you going to hurt my people?" He demanded of her. He was fiercely protective of his pack, and, as his luck would have it, that was probably the single most thing that Analise respected about him.

She gave him a firm and studious look for what seemed like an eternity. Scrutiny and desperation rolled up into one pathetic expression. "Are you joking?" She asked after desperation finally seemed to win. "Rhys, I can barely move. What the hell am I going to do to anyone?"

"By this time next week you'll be feeling fine," he told her flatly. "And compassionate and understanding aren't two words I'd use to describe you. Nor grateful, for that matter," he added a bit bitterly. Isa was right. He should have killed her.

Analise's eyes flashed with injury and they wearily searched his for a moment. "That's not true," she countered, obvious hurt in her tone. "That guy... he... " For the very first time since they had met, Analise broke off eye contact. "I'm grateful."

Rhys frowned. He hadn't meant to be so harsh with her. "Well then I suppose you'll be happy to hear that I killed him," he reported with enough coldness to match

Shepherd any day of the week.

"...Why would that make me happy?" She answered in an almost hollow voice. "I became an FBI agent to stop all of this chaotic violence and injustice, not to revel in it just because I was wronged."

Rhys blinked a few times in disbelief but Shepherd continued. "Yeah," she said finally, "Emotionally that makes me pretty happy and in that context I'll never be able to repay you for it. I'm glad that fucker is dead and I shouldn't admit that I hope it was violent and painful." Of course if had been both of those. "But justice goes beyond my hurt. It's a balance in the system so that represents true fairness. It's pure balance, independent of emotion. It's why justice is blind. It hears only facts and weighs them against one another to find the truth. Marek earned his death. He should have been tried first."

Rhys raised both eyebrows and nearly laughed at her in spite of himself. In a way, what she said was very admirable, but it didn't apply to werewolves in the slightest. "By a jury of his peers, I suppose?"

Analise's frown slid into further depth. "Are you mocking me?" She asked genuinely.

"Not intentionally, no," he answered. "Things... things work differently for us. He was an alpha. A rogue. He was challenging my territory and harming people under my care. He knew the potential consequences of his actions and did them anyway. Independent of any other laws, he broke the laws of our kind the moment he entered my land without notification. Challenging the authority of an alpha leads to a death."

Analise's eyes remained fixed on the ceiling. "...how many people have you killed?"

The question was so clinical but it put Rhys on edge right away. "I..." He couldn't answer the question.

"I've killed eight," she said after Rhys couldn't figure out how to answer the question. "They were all in self-defense. A junky pulling a gun. That sort of thing. I've never tried to justify those deaths with some explanation of how they deserved to die." Analise turned her head to direct an exhausted glare at Rhys's direction. "And you're worried that I am going to hurt your family?"

Rhys didn't know what to say. He figured that he should have been comforted, given what she implied, but instead he found himself feeling dirty. Tainted. This concept of justice of hers was beyond the sort of thing he ever thought about. He had no idea whether or not she was even right. How could he debate her in such a thing?

Analise turned her eyes back toward the ceiling. "If I understand you correctly, then I'm guessing you and yours aren't connected with the kidnappings," she said with finality. "Of course you realize I will be investigating this, but as a gesture of gratitude, I'll keep it quiet so as not to involve your innocent with my people. They... they won't be very understanding about it." That was an understatement, but that she was volunteering to keep things quiet went a long way to putting Rhys more at ease.

"The people you've killed is a local matter," she continued. "It's not within my jurisdiction to investigate those matters and for the sake of my own sanity, I'm going to assume that these deaths were similar to the situation you rescued me from." The words caught Rhys's attention. Rescue. He wouldn't have ever thought Analise to be the sort in need of being rescued and while she had been, it spoke well of her that she so easily admitted that it was in fact the nature of the situation. The wolf inside of Rhys growled in delight at what it perceived to be the smallest hint of submission out of this woman.

"In such a context, I'm going to assume that if they pertained to anything other than werewolves you'd have reported and thoroughly documented each instance. I don't want to know if I'm wrong."

"I'm going to need your help in my report," she said with a sigh. "Being sick isn't against the law. You're free to practice whatever religion you want. If I understand you correctly, then you've been sheltering Riverton from this insanity which is the same thing I've been trying to do my whole life. Sounds to me like we're on the same page on this one, Rhys," she let out. "Unfortunately, you're the only ones of your kind who aren't raving lunatics in the whole country. There's no way my superiors are going to believe me no matter how logical I make it read." Analise couldn't believe she was asking for his help, but then, she was in way over her head and knew it.

Rhys let out an obviously relieved sigh. He had many faults, but his one strength was his ability to talk to people. Throughout the worst of it, it was that trait that had kept his pack's morale from completely disintegrating. It also probably brokered the most important peace treaty his pack would ever know. "Whatever you need," he answered, notably more at ease.

"Is there a cure for this?" She asked with a hint of fragility in her voice. From her knowledge of this, she already knew the answer.

Any excitement he had been feeling was gone again. "No." he answered flatly. "Not one I know about," he added. "I'd have taken it years ago if there were." Rhys let out a bit of a sigh. He had never before told anyone what he had just admitted to and the sad truth of it was, he was completely honest. He often day dreamed about what it would be like to just be normal and not have to worry with most of the things that kept him up at night.

"I should probably let you rest," he suggested. "Allison said she wanted to come in and thank you later, for what you did to save her and the other girls... If you want."

"Did they bite them too?"

Rhys was silent. It was answer enough.

"What's going to happen to them?"

"They're home with their families for right now," he told her truthfully. Analise was skeptical but didn't argue. "I already spoke with Paul, Allison's pop, and explained some of what's going to start happening with her. My guess is they'll keep her at home until she graduates high school. She'll probably join up with us after that." "So what is going to start happening to them?" Analise asked hesitantly.

Rhys arched an eyebrow at her. "Your internal organs and bones are being restructured," he explained gently. "It's the only way you'll survive the shift. Something about an end on your DNA too. The thing that makes you age. Your genes are being altered; you won't age like you used to."

"How does that work?"

Rhys shrugged. "Can't really say," he answered. "I was born this way. It's always been a second nature to me. I can ask one of the new girls to explain her experiences to you, if you think it will help."

Analise was having trouble keeping her eyes opened. "Am I going to be a different person?"

No one had ever asked Rhys that before. "I... I don't think so. You'll be more aggressive. I know that. There will be some animal instincts too." He was quiet for a moment. "You're going to become a wolf," he answered finally. Analise winced again but said nothing. "You'll be a superposition of a wolf and yourself. I can't say what the wolf side will be like, but the Analise side should stay pretty much the same."

"Where am I? There are going to be a lot of questions..."

"You're in a special wing of Riverton Medical that handles this sort of thing," he told her finally. "Right now, the doctors are reporting that you're in critical condition but making good progress. They'll move you out to recovery after you've finished the change."

Analise was drifting. She only had a few more minutes of consciousness left. "I need my computer," she told him weakly. "I need to start the report... There's going to be a lot of questions... The girls are still in danger... After he left the room, Rhys quickly convened the pack and reported the news; that he had successfully talked the werewolf hunter down from pursuing the pack, and in fact, she was interested in helping to protect them to a certain degree. It was something of an exaggeration, of course, but Rhys hadn't seen so much relief since thirty years' prior when the omega males heard the news that they would be able to find mates. Rhys was actually a bit surprised by it all. He had been so busy trying to resolve these issues that he hadn't been around to experience the anxiety in the pack. All around him were announcements that they were safe, that the scare was over, that things would be even better now. He had frowned slightly at this. He wasn't sure that the worst hadn't yet come.

Analise was barely conscious for long enough to hold any sort of conversation in the days that followed and Rhys decided it was best to give her some space to cope with everything that had happened. In truth, he wasn't sure if it was her or him who needed the space more. And so, Harvey's return from France couldn't have been better timed and he handed the issue off to his younger brother, hoping that it would help him focus more on his work. Of course, it hadn't. Harvey had been hinting that things weren't going well and that he was having to give her drugs to help her sleep.

While this had disturbed Rhys, he hadn't fully considered it. His mind was busy elsewhere. Something she had said to him truly bothered him. It was her comment about the people she had killed. They had all been in self-defense, but if he had understood her correctly, Analise did not believe that they deserved death. She honestly preferred a trial to the fate she had administered.

At first, Rhys thought this was foolish. Anyone who was stupid enough to attack him was asking for death. It was a given. If Analise was to become some super werewolf type, then this would be the same for her. Analise had even confirmed what Isa had said; that she would show her enemies no mercy.

Why then did it bother him that her ideas of justice impacted her this way? The more he thought, the more distracted he became by it. He had never once even questioned the deaths of the people he had killed. Analise was correct in her assumptions. Rhys had killed many times in his life, but it had always been in defense of his pack. If it had not been werewolf related, he would have reported it and handled it appropriately.

But to question whether they should have died? That had never occurred to him. A werewolf truly was a superposition of a wolf and a man. The wolf was just that; an animal, or so Rhys believed. Animals did not question the act of killing prey or even threats to their territory and Rhys's wolf was particularly brutal at times.

Analise's wolf was yet to be seen, but it would be an animal all the same. Animals didn't have regret. There was no concept of justice. That was a human concept.

And so, Rhys sat at his temporary desk staring at the wall as he pondered thoughts that were much deeper than anything he had considered in decades. This certainly wasn't the time for distractions, either. The attack on the precinct meant loads of paper work and the obvious media misdirection. There were mourning coworkers to deal with, and worse, the FBI was constantly demanding information on the retrieval of the girls, the cult, and Analise's condition.

Two days after the woman was hospitalized, a pair of agents showed up and set up shop in the conference room on the second floor of City Hall, sifting through Analise's notes and generally making themselves a nuisance. If he had thought Analise was arrogant, it was nothing compared to these two. Agent Peters, the taller of the two men, refused to talk to anyone but Rhys, and even then, it was only ever to send him on some demeaning errand, like making copies or fetching coffee. Agent Carter, on the other hand, was constantly explaining basic law enforcement knowledge to Rhys as if he didn't have a clue.

There was no doubt that Analise thought herself an expert, but at least she made an effort to include Rhys on her findings from the start rather than talking to him like a servant. He had to wonder, given what he knew now about her, if some of her previous behavior wasn't due to training rather than inherent snobbery.

Carter was irritating, but it was Peters who was the one that had Rhys worried. He rarely spoke, but when he did, he asked questions that obviously implied Peters had more intimate knowledge of weres than Analise did. Rhys found himself hoping her change would happen soon so she could take care of these men and get out of his hair. All of this interaction with the Bureau was decidedly bad for his pack, High Alpha potential aside.

"NO!" Came the impassioned protest of Harvey from down the hall. Rhys had nearly forgotten that his brother had returned the same day Analise was admitted to the hospital.

Rhys let out a short sigh. This was probably going to push him over the edge. If Harvey was here it meant things at the Hospital were bad and that Harvey was about to let him down. Nothing was ever easy. "Now get the hell outta my way! Where is- damn it Rhys!" He let out in complete frustration as he burst into Rhys's make-shift office in City Hall.

Rhys offered Harvey a frown. Harv still had his lab coat on. The messy hair and tired eyes looked about the same way Rhys felt. Harvey's jaw was tight as he pushed his way into the office without being invited. Normally Rhys would have tolerated it, but things were far too hectic for this. "Get out," He ordered his brother.

"Absolutely not!" Harvey returned. "That woman is a nightmare. You are going to listen to me and stop ignoring my calls or we-"

Rhys had thrown the punch before Harvey could finish the thought. It landed perfectly on Harvey's jaw, tossing the man backward into the wall. "I told you to get out," he stated, barely able to keep himself from shifting due to anger. "You have a job to do now get out and go do it."

Harv's eyes flared as his own rage surfaced. Harvey leaped forward, barreling into Rhys like a linebacker, sending the two of them backward into Rhys's desk. Rhys turned midair and slammed Harvey face first into the papers that were scattered across the surface. "I can't do it!" Harvey shouted furiously. "She's resisting and it's too painful for her. She's been trying to shift for a week and won't let it out."

"You told me it would be fast and painless you son of a bitch," Rhys hissed at his brother. "What the fuck am I supposed to tell those dicks on the second floor, huh? Oh excuse me, agent, while me and the other werewolves keep your injured agent drugged so she doesn't scream herself to sleep from the pain of turning into one of us?!" "I'm doing everything I can!" Harvey protested as Rhys held him furiously down to the desk. He was morbidly curious if Rhys was going to kill him. He'd never seen his brother this furious before.

Rhys tossed him to the floor, glowering over him. "Bullshit," He hissed.

Harvey rubbed his jaw, but didn't try to get up. Rhys would likely not hold back and Harvey knew he couldn't take him even if his heart was in it. "Last I checked, I was the one with the medical degree, dick face," he answered hotly. "She won't listen to anyone. I want to put her down. This is sick. As a doctor, I can't put her through this pain and if she won't listen to me..."

Rhys's expression told Harvey that his timing was bad. Rhys clenched his fists as he bared down on his brother. His expression had darkened. "Do I need to go down there." He more stated than asked. His voice was gravelly with anger.

"Yes." Harvey answered firmly. He wasn't about to let Rhys see how intimidated he was in that moment. "You're the only one she'll listen to. Half the nurses are ready to quit on me. I can't keep her sedated any more. She's about to change but she won't listen... "

Rhys grabbed his coat furiously and slammed the door behind him, leaving Harvey on the floor in his office. The glass in the window shattered from the force of he delivered to the door. He was silently grateful it was the door and not his brother. This absolutely wasn't what he needed. Harvey had one job. One job. He just had to see Analise through the change and he was probably the best qualified for it in the whole pack. Rhys really didn't think he was asking that much and in all honesty, Brody and Isa were supposed to be helping too. Rhys had even assigned Harvey's poodle to the situation once he got wind that things weren't going well but from what he had heard, Clarise (the French woman's real name), was so offended she was threatening to return to France just days after arriving.

He needed them to keep things quiet so he could keep the two new Agents busy long enough for Analise to heal up. It was all they had to do and between the four of them, their solution was to send Harvey to him threatening to put her down? Rhys's anger was fully justified. It was a transparent ploy. Rhys wouldn't kill Harvey, but the others weren't guaranteed that sort of familial safety net. That, and Harvey could take the beating Rhys had in store for him.

"You had one fucking job," He muttered in anger as he hopped into the beat up old pick up, slamming the door. He didn't even care who saw him in that moment. Sure, he was over reacting, but the outlet for the stress was actually welcomed.

Rhys tried to calm down as he pulled into the parking lot of Riverton Medical. It wasn't a very big hospital, but the Healing Center was an isolated ward all the same. Sometimes people had trouble with their change or someone in the pack would develop a rather Lichen related illness and it was best to keep these things out of view from the humans. The two federal agents sitting in the vacant office down town were testimony enough to support the wisdom in that choice.

This was why Rhys's frown intensified as he walked into the hospital to be greeted to the muted sounds of Analise screaming in agony. The receptionist sitting at the admissions desk was white faced. Apparently this had been going on for a while. Rhys didn't bother explaining himself, nor did he have to. Everyone, it seemed, knew that the Chief of Medicine had gone to fetch his brother for this one and given the situation, no one was going to question the Captain of the police force running toward the sound of the screams.

And that was precisely what Rhys did. He was running toward the Healing Center before he even stopped to think. The horrified faces only grew more intense as he approached. Brody was waiting outside Analise's room and he jumped to his feet as Rhys came into the hallway. He was healing quickly from the attack, though his leg was now in a walking brace. "Now Rhys" he started, trying to intercept the larger man who was obviously on a war path.

Rhys's patience was shot and his fist found Brody's nose before the beta stood a chance of slowing him down. Brody recoiled slightly and stepped away as

Rhys burst into the room. Clarise and Isa were trying desperately to hold Analise still while her body contorted with sickening sounds of cracking bones that shifted to and from human form into the hybrid form of the wolf. It was surprising that the woman was still conscious, given the pain she was almost certainly enduring.

Rhys did not pause as he took the scene in, though it would haunt him for the rest of his life. Analise was resisting the change at great physical pain. It was best to let the shift happen as quickly as possible. The first change was always the worst, and even more so for humans who were unaccustomed. Still, they had always been educated on what would happen and embraced this as something to be desired. Analise's change had not been consensual, and, she was too strong willed for her own good.

Isa turned as Rhys entered and opened her mouth to speak, but Rhys interrupted her. "GET OUT NOW!" He bellowed at the women, who both would have tucked their tails and retreated if they were in wolf form. They didn't require further instruction and were out of the room in a heartbeat.

Rhys's sense of propriety was lost and he jumped onto the bed pinning Analise down and firmly grasping her head in his hands, forcing her eyes to look into his. She was terrified, that much was obvious. In great panic, her green eyes darted back and forth between his, searching for some measure of comfort.

"Let it happen," he ordered her firmly. That he wasn't shouting at her was about as much comfort as he could offer her. "Stop resisting it, Analise!"

"Nnnnoooo," she managed to get out in a voice that couldn't decide between human or wolf. She struggled to break free of his grip, but her body was essentially convulsing as it embodied the confusion of forms.

"Why?" He demanded. "You can't stop this from happening! You're only going to hurt yourself."

"I don't want to be an animal," she let out as tears spilled out of her eyes.

Rhys paused only momentarily from surprise. That was a new one. Analise was terrified of her inner wolf and was violently fighting for control. What she refused to understand was that fighting the wolf was only making the wolf fight harder. Apparently they were both incredibly stubborn and the battle being waged for control over their shared body was probably the most epic war he had ever witnessed.

Rhys himself started to panic for a brief moment when he realized that Analise wasn't going to back down and the two of them were going to end up self-destructing. It was like a scary story werewolves told their children to keep them obedient about shifting. No one resisted a shift; it meant the most painful and agonizing death imaginable. "No fucking shit," he answered in exasperated surprise. "God damn it, Analise, you're gonna kill yourself."

Her eyes widened slightly in momentary terror. He didn't think anything could scare that woman, though, this ordeal was certainly frightening him. The pack wouldn't turn any humans for a few decades after news of this one got around. Rhys tightened his grip on her hair and pulled her face forward to only an inch or two away from his. He used his strength to hold her as firmly as possible, though it was obvious that her inner wolf was quite powerful. "Listen to me," he told her, panic starting to surface in his voice. "You're still Analise, you understand me? You're still Analise and nothing is going to change that. I'm right here. I'm not going anywhere. You've gotta let this wolf out, Analise, or she's going to kill you."

"I don... I dun wanna eat yo," her speech was slurring between growls and intelligible words.

"You aren't," he assured her. "I'm gonna shift as soon as you do, ok? My wolf is bigger than yours; I won't let you hurt anyone but you gotta let her out or she'll rip you apart." He was bluffing. He had no idea how big Analise's wolf would be and judging by the power that was seeping through, it may very well be a close match; something that was only serving to intimidate him.

"Bettr me than yo," she gurgled out.

"Damn it woman please for once just listen to me," he pleaded with her. "You gotta keep it together! I've got two agents who won't leave until they see you alive and well. So just let it out! We'll deal with how to fix it later."

"WHAT?" She answered in horrified surprise. "Pertres?" It was as close to Peters as she could say. Rhys nodded once, now having trouble holding her still.

Analise's panic grew into complete chaos. That response did nothing to instill confidence in Rhys. He was already worried that Peters was the sharp one and a terrified Analise only served to confirm that hunch. The tears were freely streaming from her eyes at this point. There was nothing she wouldn't have done to avoid this fate, but unfortunately for her, it was inevitable. "Plss help me," she stammered out.

"LET IT OUT ANALISE!" He all but screamed at her. "I swear to god I'll keep you safe just let it out before you rip yourself to shreds."

She couldn't hold out any longer. All it took was a moment for her to consider Rhys's request and the wolf took hold. The force of the wolf bursting into control was sufficient to send Rhys hurling backward as a large brown wolf exploded into existence, tearing through the hospital gown and bed sheets with a loud and agonized howl.

Rhys collided with the wall behind him, but scarcely missed a beat. The wolf was utterly disoriented and her unsure paws slid along the floor like a dog on slippery ice. In terror, the wolf pushed herself under the hospital bed, looking more like a cornered cat than the great wolf that she was.

Rhys didn't even pause as Analise skid to an awkward landing beneath the bed, trembling from the horrible pain she had been enduring. Rhys ripped off his clothes as fast as he could, shifting in an instant as he had promised.

Not that Analise would have known, but Rhys avoided shifting as much as possible. This was one rare occasion when his human form demanded the services of the beast for something other than killing an opponent. Rhys slowly trotted up to the bed, crouching down to make eye contact with Analise. She was whining from the pain and offered Rhys a mild yelp as he came into view. It would take her a while to learn how to retain some of her human faculties in wolf form. For now, the Analise he knew would be buried in there, watching helplessly from the wolf's eyes, just as the wolf had been forced to do when Analise was in charge. The two of them were going to have to work out some sort of arrangement to share their body.

That was one argument Rhys was Suite glad to not be involved in.

Two green eyes found his from the safety of her haven. He eased forward slightly, causing Analise to back a bit into the wall. She was still whimpering and trembling terribly from the pain. He inched forward again, taking in as much of her scent as he could and examining her new form.

Analise was an enormous wolf. She was just as tall as Rhys and possibly longer than he was, though rather than the bulk that he carried in wolf form, she was lean and sleek. Her legs were long and her torso was far more narrow than his. If he had to guess, what she lacked in strength she would more than make up for in speed and agility. In a fair fight, they would be evenly matched. As it presently stood, she didn't have sufficient space for her speed to counter his strength.

Rhys would be able to hold true to his promise. In this setting, he could dominate her and keep her isolated here until Analise was able to re-conquer the wolf and shift back. Rhys's wolf was in control of this situation in more ways than this, however. From behind his wolf eyes, Rhys was shocked to realize that his wolf was intent on mating with Analise once she was recovered. His wolf saw her as an equal, something he almost never experienced, and this was the first time he saw an equal in someone other than an opponent. The kinship the wolf felt for her was instant and deep. As a wolf, she was striking. Her fur was a deep chestnut color, gradually blending into mahogany socks and a deep mahogany muzzle. Her tail was bushier than most, almost like a fox, and her fir was sleek.

Rhys couldn't hold the wolf back as he inched forward to nuzzle against her snout with his own maw in a surprisingly affectionate way. Much to his surprise, Analise's wolf did not try to nip or attack. Instead, she nuzzled back, seeking comfort from a friendly wolf in her moment of great pain. She was hesitant and confused, but receptive to Rhys's presence. Slowly, he moved forward until he had wrapped himself around her, spooning along beside her as she rested and drifted to sleep. Rhys didn't move and wouldn't. He and his wolf were in agreement that they would stay by her side, though obviously for entirely different reasons. Once this had calmed down, he and Isa were going to have to have some words. For now, the wolf was thoroughly enjoying a rare moment of intimacy, rather than only being let out to kill.

Before Rhys himself drifted into a peaceful sleep, he considered what Analise had said. She didn't want to be an animal. Perhaps that was what he was for denying his wolf such a simple pleasure as company for all these years. Analise's physical agony was all because she refused to accept what she was. Was that really any different than Rhys and the depth of his loneliness?

Even as a born wolf, had he every truly embraced what he was?

What did it mean to be a werewolf?

It was sometime later when Analise finally awoke from beneath their hospital bed. Every muscle in her body ached painfully and she was sleeping on the cold tile floor. The only warmth she felt was coming from the body curled up behind her.

She blinked a few times, unsure if she were Analise again or that animal that was lurking inside of her. It had been a terrible experience and no one had bothered to explain that part. Turn into a wolf, they said. It'll be fast and painless, they said. Fucking liars. I should gut every last one of them she found herself thinking darkly.

Analise frowned slightly. Gutting people was not her usual internal threat of choice. Usually she promised to punch someone in the face or kick them in the balls. Something a little less... gory.

She let out a small, pathetic sigh at her plight and to her surprise, a strong arm wrapped tightly around her, pulling her closer into the warm body. Her eyes thrust widely open as she realized that not only was she apparently sleeping with someone under the bed, they were both naked.

Rhys. Oh god... What the hell happened?

Letting out a gasp, she tried to roll over and push away as quickly as she could. Instead, she merely let out a gasp. Her muscles were far too painful for anything as acrobatic as rolling, apparently, and pushing was definitely out of the question. Rhys's deep cobalt blue eyes blinked open in confusion. He settled his eyes instantly on Analise's, resulting in more confusion before propriety set in and he slid back slightly, reaching the same arm that had embraced her up and over the bed to retrieve a blanket for her.

"Did... Did we..." Her eyes were still as wide as quarters as she brought arms across her chest.

"Mate?" He answered in perhaps the least romantic way possible as he tugged the blanket down and started draping it around her. She was visibly quite grateful for that. "I don't think so," he answered quietly. It was clear that Rhys was exhausted and probably could have used a few more hours of sleep.

"You don't think so?" She repeated incredulously.

He offered her a tired chuckle. "Wolf fell asleep sometime after yours finally did," he answered quietly again. "I didn't even realize I shifted back," he added curiously. That had never happened before, but he decided not to tell her that. He eyed her cautiously. "You ok?"

She blinked a few times in disbelief, adjusting the blanket for modesty. "I..." Shepherd just let it go and sigh apathetically. The obvious answer was no, no she wasn't ok, but then, there really was no point in belaboring the issue any more. "They said it wasn't going to hurt," she finally answered.

Rhys frowned. "I've never seen a turn go that badly before," he told her, rolling to his back and resting his head on his arm as he stared absently at the bed springs. "Looks like you're both incredibly stubborn and persistent. Guess I already knew you were like that."

"They also said I'd be in control the entire time," she continued in the same quiet voice.

Rhys chuckled a bit. "Yeah... doesn't really work that way."

Analise was not sharing his humor in this. "How does it work? There's no way in hell I'm letting that happen again."

"I don't advise that," Rhys warned, his humor feigning slightly. "She'll rip you apart to get out." He let out a sigh and turned to look at her slightly. "You want to get out from under here?" Analise was shivering, probably from the cold floor, but her eyes were locked on his with an intense demand for information.

The question snapped her back to her surroundings. "Yeah... I... where are our clothes?" she asked out loud.

Rhys smirked again. He wasn't sure why he was enjoying this side of her so much. It was likely because she seemed so naive and ignorant. That definitely wasn't a trait he thought he'd see from her, but she carried it well enough. He had half expected her to shrug off her lack of knowledge and pretend she had expected all of this. It was then that he realized he had grossly misunderstood her.

Analise wasn't arrogant, she was confident and intelligent. If she was a man he wouldn't have questioned it at all. In a woman, he hadn't been expecting that combination.

Rhys slid out from under the bed and then peered under, offering her a hand. One hand remained tightly clutched to the hospital blanket for propriety and the other hesitantly reached out to accept the help.

She winced as she finally slid out and propped herself up. Muscles she didn't even know she had were on fire for just the slightest of movements. Her eyes casually drifted over to Rhys before she instantly snapped her gaze away again. "Jesus, Rhys!" She reprimanded slightly. He, obviously, was not at all shy about nudity.

Rhys chuckled again as he tugged on his worn blue jeans. "Clothes are a human thing," he explained. "Uncontrolled shifting has a way of... well destroying them. But I'd get used to it, if I were you. I think our wolves are friends," he added through a grin. Analise was sure to hate that part.

Analise was beet red from embarrassment and offered him a sour look. "Fantastic," she offered dryly. "What other fun surprises to I have in store? I mean, uncontrolled shifting just sounds lovely."

Rhys padded over and scooped her up, replacing her in the bed, before moving over to pull a side chair over. Analise tugged her knees up into her chest as she pulled herself into a sitting position. "You are sharing your body with a female wolf," he explained gently. "If it helps, she's just as confused as you are right now, I'd figure." "That doesn't help," she answered flatly. "How do I kill it?"

Rhys was horrified. "You don't," he answered sharply. "And you best not repeat that again."

She sulked slightly in reply. "I don't want to be an animal," she offered almost pathetically.

"Well neither did I." The words were out of his mouth before he really thought about it. "I didn't exactly have a choice in the matter either. Don't mean you have to kill her just because she's not convenient," he added through a deep frown.

Analise blinked a few times, "Sorry," she offered, genuinely so. "I... I'm sorry. That wasn't very nice I guess... "

Rhys shrugged and rubbed his face. "You're going to have to figure out how to get along," he advised seriously. "And keeping her locked away all the time isn't going to work. She needs let out every now and then."

"So... It's like... a pet?" The poor woman was extremely confused but the question caused Rhys to smirk.

"Not exactly," he replied. "More like a sister, but if pet works, you may as well try it." Analise leaned her head back and closed her eyes. For a brief moment, Rhys just studied her in silence. "His name is Aru," he said finally. "My wolf." Rhys shrugged, adding, "I've never told anyone that, though, so I'd appreciate if it stayed between us."

Analise opened her eyes and cocked a curious eyebrow at him. "Then why are you telling me?"

"Might help," he offered. "Besides, Aru likes your wolf and she was receptive to him being around. That's not real common for him."

Analise looked confused again and shook her head slightly. "Wait, is this some weird third person conversation. I'm lost." Rhys chuckled and shook his head in reply but Analise continued before he could articulate. "Look, Rhys, you're a really nice guy. Obviously attractive -"

"Oh obviously?" He answered though the grin and a chuckle.

"Yeah, well, look, I'm a mess -"

"Oh I know," Rhys interrupted. "I've been seriously considering killing you a couple times, if you'll recall."

She opened her mouth to retort and paused. "This is the strangest conversation I've ever had," she finally admitted with her standard dry humor.

"Look, if it helps, I really am talking for Aru and your wolf. See, part of the way this works is through compromise. You remember that, don't you? Team work?"

"Oh yes, our magical temporary arrangement to facilitate catching the bad guys," she answered. Rhys was decidedly enjoying her dry humor. Most everyone he knew would never prod him so much, though Harvey was known to on occasion.

"Well, you and her are going to have to practice that idea," he advised. "Life will be easier on you both if you do."

Analise sighed heavily and resumed leaning her head back against the wall. "You said Agent Peters is here or was I hallucinating that?"

Rhys frowned at the change in subject. "Yeah him and a guy named Carter," he answered. It was back to business, it seemed.

Analise nodded. "Carter's fine. Peters is trouble," she answered almost cryptically. "What did you tell them about me?"

"That you were assaulted and beaten. Hospital records have you recovering in ICU with no visitors until you officially wake up," he responded, getting up to fetch his shirt and boots.

Analise frowned, rubbing the bridge of her nose. "Ok. Move me out of here today and let Carter know. And I'm going to need to see my medical records and all my files too," she added.

Rhys flashed her a stern frown. Which caused Analise to appear contemplative. "You know... this is really strange but... I feel like I should be saying please but every time I'm about to, something tells me it's the wrong thing to say..." A sense of alarm crossed her eyes. "Seriously, what the hell is going on with me? You said I'd be the same person."

"Yeah but a little more aggressive," he answered with a sharp sigh. "And you just tell that "something" that that's yet to be seen," he added, nearly growling.

"See... now I'm wanting to bite you," she told him with an appropriately place eye roll. "Definitely not something normal me does. I think you better go and send in that doctor of yours for me to yell at before I start acting on that urge," she said with the same dry humor.

CHAPTER 4

It was enough for Rhys to crack a smile. "Agent Peters has been holed up in an office for the last week reading who couldn't have been out of her teens stormed down your reports," he told her. The amused smirk slid into a real and genuine concern. "That's what I thought," Rhys said through a sigh. "... I can tell them that you didn't ever wake up," he offered seriously. He knew what that would mean for her. Her entire world would be over if she faked her death.

Analise shook her head and forced a smile. "He's too sharp for it," she answered as confidently as she could. "Let me worry about those two," she concluded. "but uh... it might not be a bad idea to get those girls away from here. He doesn't have any reason to believe that your family is involved in this, but if he's been reading my notes..." she didn't finish her thought, though she didn't have to. The four girls who they had rescued were still in danger.

Rhys nodded and left the room. Brody was sitting outside the room and looked up at Rhys apologetically. He was about to say something when a young woman who couldn't have been out of her teens stormed down the hall on a war path. Unlike Brody, Starla's eyes were locked firmly on Rhys's. She was confident in this for longer than Rhys was expecting and he cocked a curious eyebrow at her as she stomped forward and slapped Rhys had across the face.

The blow did nothing to him, but Brody was out of his seat holding Starla back before Rhys had scarcely blinked. "They were just trying to help!" She shouted furiously at Rhys.

"You're siding with that wolf hunter over your own brother? Over Brod!? What the hell's gotten into you!"

"I'm sorry," Brody kept blurting out as he tried to get the little ball of anger under control and out of the hall way. The ruckus echoed down the hallways for quite a way, leaving Rhys to watch in the general direction while scratching his head.

Isa stepped up behind him then, walking ever silently and purposefully. Rhys turned to regard her, but mostly, he was interested in her take on this. To his surprise, Isa did not have her usual supportive expression on. "News of the turn has spread," she reported in a tired voice. "It is unlikely we will turn another human for many years."

Rhys frowned. "It was pretty bad," he admitted in his standard General Rhys voice.

"The failure was yours and hers," Isa replied solidly. "It was not ours. She is a High Alpha."

Rhys's frown hardened and he approached Isa in an aggressive fashion, backing her instantly into a wall. "I can't be everywhere at once," he snapped angrily. "You're telling me that the four of you couldn't figure out how coach a human through a turn? With, what? Fifty such turns under your belt in the last few years? Whose bright idea was it to lie to her about the control issue? Or the pain? You seem to know so much about High Alpha's, Isa. What did you think something like her was going to do when she realized you were lying to her? Or were you counting on her resisting until she tore herself apart?"

His eyes would have burned through hers if they could. There was no apology on Isa's face. It had been she who had advocated killing Analise. He wasn't terribly surprised that she would make one final pass at it, though it did disappoint him a bit. He pulled away before she could answer, turning to walk down the hall toward Harvey's office. "Get her some clothes and get her moved to the main hospital."

Meanwhile...

"You told me I would be zee dominant female," Clarise hissed at Harvey from behind the office door. Her light blue eyes were scalding hot as she glared furiously at Rhys's younger brother. "I did not leave France just to be subordinate to you American wolves!"

"No, you left France to marry me," Harvey countered firmly. "Are you telling me that this is just a ploy to position yourself?"

Clarise was silent.

"She's not going to stay long," Harvey stated as if it were the gospel truth.

Harvey could almost hear Clarise rolling her eyes. "Don't be absurd," she scoffed. "She will stay for Rhys."

Harvey chuckled. "I doubt that."

"How can you be so blind!" She hissed emphatically. "Can you really not smell her pheromones? It is disgusting!"

"Obviously they have you females all worked up," Harvey offered through a chuckle. "They won't work on Rhys, though," he said dismissively.

Clarise slammed her fist on his desk in anger. "Stop your senseless hero worship, Harvey! He is not immune to her just because he is your brozer!"

"Of course not," Harvey answered calmly. Harvey shook his head sadly as he offered her a pleasant smile. "Let me explain something, Clarise. Rhys isn't some run of the mill Alpha male. This world is full of examples of those and look what's happened. How many packs were hunted to extinction because of what the average Alpha male did? Your own pack was destroyed because of it."

"What are you saying?" Clarise asked incredulously. "Your pack went into hiding razer zan fighting like-"

"Like a bunch of rabid fools," Harvey finished for her. His light hearted tone was starting to evaporate. "In an era when the large packs are being exterminated and the future of our race is reduced to gypsy rogues, my brother listened to the needs and wisdom of his pack rather than asserting his dominance on us like some tyrant and what happened? We're the only pack in the world that saw actual growth after the decree went out.

We're one of the few American packs that aren't on the FBI's watch list. Hell, the FBI is here and they haven't found us."

Harvey leaned forward and rested his elbows on his knees. "He should have killed her the second she showed up. It's what any other alpha would have done. It's what Isa wanted him to do. Instead, he convinced the werewolf hunter to defend us. That's never been done before. Ever. In the history of our existence, no wolf has ever talked a hunter down, let alone convinced one to fight on our behalf instead. Don't you get it? There's nothing average about Rhys at all."

A tense silence fell between them. "He is not a High Alpha, Harvey. You are delusional if you honestly believe zat."

Harvey simply shook his head sadly at her. "Come on, Clarise. You're smarter than this. Do you actually think I have any respect for the High Alphas at all after everything that's happened?" Harvey chuckled again. "High Alphas have an important role in our society, no doubt about it, but to assume that they should be our ultimate leaders who aren't to be questioned is antiquated. If our race's history has shown us anything, it's that the humans always win in any conflict with them. We can win battles, but the war is always theirs and they wipe us out for our efforts. Why then, would anyone have thought kidnapping their daughters was going to end any differently? It was the council who decreed this action. It was High Alphas and almost everyone followed them blindly to their doom."

"No, Clarise, the time of the High Alphas is over. Rhys just spat in their faces when this little experiment of ours actually worked. He's no High Alpha and thank god for that."

Clarise rolled her eyes slightly, though it was obvious that she was starting to consider Harvey's position. "And don't you zink zere will be consequences for zat?" She countered. "Besides, you are again being too generous. From what I have heard, zis was Isa's idea, not Rhys's"

Harvey shrugged. "Doesn't mean he had to listen to her. He's in charge, not her. I had the idea to kill Analise when she refused to turn but he didn't go with it. Besides, just because Isa had the idea for it doesn't mean she was the one who had to make it all happen. It was mostly Rhys." He let out a bit of a concerned sigh. "As for the consequences... yeah, I think there will be. Something about all of this; the rogue pack coming and kidnapping those girls, the FBI showing up... there's even a rumor that one of the women in the strays we can't find is Analise's sister... something doesn't feel right."

Harvey was quiet for a moment. When he did speak again, it was with an authority he almost never used. "And when something does happen, it will be our little High Alpha werewolf hunter who's going to go take care of it. Rhys won't let her go alone. When she leaves, and she will leave, Rhys will be leaving with her."

Clarise looked surprised at this, now starting to see where Harvey was headed. "You just got done convincing me zat we need him... " she started.

Harvey looked over at Clarise. "What we need to do is demonstrate to Rhys that the pack is safe in our hands. I've known the man for almost a hundred years and only in the last month have I ever seen him delegate any of his responsibility. This is the first time he's ever trusted me to do anything without him, and I just fucked it all up," Harvey reported, his tone slightly sad again.

"But see, Clar, you're used to taking care of yourself and we need someone like that around here." He smiled gently at her. "I wasn't lying to you when I promised you'd be the alpha female. You just got to be a little more patient is all. That, and, make nice with Analise so Rhys trusts you enough to hand things over to you when that time comes."

Clarise didn't know what to say. Most of her anger was completely gone. She looked over to Harvey almost apologetically, but with a degree of wonder as well. Harvey had offered her the world that she had wanted. While all of these men had been literally chasing her tail for the last fifty years, it was Harvey who had bothered to learn anything about her or what dreams she may have for herself. He was so casual with her, as if the desperation that had set into all the males had somehow skipped him.

Now she was realizing that he was far more insightful than she had ever realized. He sat across from her grinning in his country boy way, offering her a set of pearly white teeth and adorable dimples. Apparently, he was also offering the alpha female status she had always wanted.

But Harvey didn't realize the full scope of it. Clarise had told him a little about her pack; about how almost all the French werewolves were wiped out after the country human girls started to go missing. France's legal system was just different enough that they had no trouble treating the were's like animals. Horrible things had been done to them at the hands of the humans. Clarise's experiences were painfully similar to Analise's from the opposite side of the same fence.

The one thing she truly wanted above all else was a safe and loving pack to take her in and Harvey was the younger brother of an alpha of just such a pack. And, Harvey had fallen in love with her at first sight, just as Clarise had done with him.

The more she considered the amazing man across from her, the harder it was for her to sit still. In a blinding flash, Clarise had vaulted from her chair and tackled Harvey to the ground, smothering his face with a rain of kisses.

For a brief moment, he was too startled to know what was happening. He just fell with her to the ground and was prone on his back as she crawled on top of him to invoke death by kissing. As her soft, delicate lips continued to brush over him, Harvey began returning her passion to match.

He reached up to cradle her head in his hands, running his fingers through her long blonde hair as he pulled her mouth deeply into his. Harvey was every bit as madly in love with this woman as she was with him. He could hardly hold back his wide grin as he started to roll over to lay atop her.

"There she is," he whispered affectionately to her. He kept one hand tangled in her hair as the other began drifting gently down her form, pausing as it ran over her large breast, before continuing downward to get under her shirt.

"I didn't trust you... I am sorry," she revealed in a soft voice. Her hands were wandering just as freely as his was and one was already pushing under the waistband of his trousers.

Harvey shook his head to dismiss the idea as he kissed her deeply again. "I don't trust me half the time either," he joked lightly. Clarise's hand slid into his trousers and her fingers had already began gently running up the length of his hard cock. The sensation caused him to grunt slightly in approval.

Simultaneously, his hand slid up her shirt until his fingers brushed across her piercing hard nipples. He allowed the points to trace across the palm of his hand as he gently fondled her breast. With each pass of her hand at his cock, Harvey was losing more and more self-control. Clarise grinned at how easily she could arouse him.

Clarise didn't need to announce when she was ready for him. The moment he had returned her kiss she had begun to moisten and now that his lips were avidly lavishing her neck while his hands worked her beautiful tits, the scent of her arousal was hanging heavily in the air.

Harvey's hips had started rocking slightly at her ministrations and he shifted his weight to tower over her even further. "Take your clothes off," He growled softly into her ear.

Clarise was already in mid-gasp when he so assertively ordered her clothes off. It was extremely arousing and she withdrew slightly to offer him hooded doe eyes of submission.

"Oh what are you doing to me?" Harvey let out in false exasperation. "So be it," He resumed his husky, dominant voice as he shifted in between her legs and ripped her panties free in a swift move. "I guess I'll just have to fuck you into obedience, my love," he promised in a hot voice.

"So be it," she whispered in return. Nothing turned her on like Harvey taking complete control of their passion.

The hot, moist air rising from her drenched pussy wrapped around Harvey's thick cock as he continued to slide in between her legs. The sensation was intoxicating and Harvey could hold back no more. Without even thinking about it, he thrust his entire length as deeply into her as he could.

Clarise let out a thoroughly pleased groan, followed by a brief whimper when he withdraw so that only the head of his dick was left inside of her. As quickly as the disappointment of emptiness found her, it was replaced by utter fullness. Harvey was taking long, purposeful strokes in and out of her as his mouth practically attached to her neck.

His hands quickly grew impatient with her blouse and in another violent gesture, he tore the shirt open, freeing her large breasts. His hands found them first, almost digging into her flesh as he gripped them tightly. Clarise let out a small cry at this but Harvey brought his mouth to hers as if to devour her passion. Her hips were already raising and lowering in tandum with his powerful thrusts.

With each stroke, they were losing themselves entirely in one another. Clarise reached behind him and tangled her hands into his hair, jerking his face downward and smashing it in between her breasts. The resulting slight spasm was indication enough that Harvey was in his own state of nirvana to be trapped against her tits. His hips thrust harder and faster until he was pumping into her like a well oiled piston.

Clarise clearly forgot that she was on the floor of Harvey's office in the hospital, but then, she could have been in the middle of time square for all it mattered. Her moaning was escalating into needful pleas for more. Harvey was not in a position to disappoint his lover.

Their bodies slapped together, each thrust rippling through Clarise so that her tits reverberated as he continued to fuck her passionately The sounds of their coupling echoed against the walls and served to punctuate her needful moaning. "I love you," He whispered hotly in her ear. Simply saying the words was enough to push him up to his limit, but it was quite effective at pushing Clarise through her first orgasm. The sensation of her tight muscles clenching and releasing his thick cock set Harvey off next.

Both Harvey and Clarise let out impassioned cries as his hot seed sprayed deeply inside of her. He collapsed atop her as soon as he was spent, panting heavily but not pulling out. There was almost certainly nothing that could happen that would cause Harvey to leave this woman and vice versa. The post coital bliss left them tangled in one another's arms, gently caressing and gasping for air. They'd likely have remained that way too, had it not been for a knock at the door...

Rhys paused as he got to the door, his hand hovering over the knob while he stood momentarily still. There was a heavy scent that he had picked up as he approached. Harvey's was one and the other one was still very new to him. Clarise. His eyes widened slightly when he realized why their scents were so strong. A devilish smirk hit him in an instant. "You old dog..." he muttered to himself in appraisal of Harvey. Rhys was weighing his options. He truly wanted to let them continue on in privacy, but, he also needed to get a hold of Shepherd's medical records before Agent Peters had a chance to do so.

Waiting until he was sure they were finished, Rhys politely tapped on the door. After a few moments of shuffle, Harvey opened the door abruptly. At first, he had the look of someone who would rip off the head of whoever dared to interrupt him in that moment. Internally Rhys smirked at this. For all his laid back intentions, Harvey was a very dominant wolf and this drove sometimes irrational levels of aggression, as Rhys well knew.

Seeing it was Rhys caused Harvey's expression to retreat slightly into an almost stoic embarrassment. "Hey Rhys," he offered delicately as he adjusted his shirt slightly. Behind him, Clarise was doing the same, running her fingers through her hair and straightening her skirt. Unlike Harvey's retreat, Clarise offered him an indignant frown.

"I didn't mean to interrupt anything," Rhys told Harvey genuinely.

"Oh no, it's ok. We were, uh... just having a little talk about Clarise moving out here more permanently," Harvey dismissed as he invited Rhys in, gesturing to one of the chairs.

"I think that would be a good idea," Rhys replied, causing Clarise to raise a curious eyebrow. He looked over at her a bit hesitantly. "I'm real sorry that we didn't have a warmer reception for you when you got here," he told her kindly. "Things have been a little crazy. Not likely to calm down anytime soon either, I suspect." He rubbed the back of his neck as he spoke to her. "Anyway, they put you up in a nice place?"

It was the wrong thing to say. Clarise seemed receptive to what she assumed was going to be an apology, but the awkward question about her accommodations caused a frown slide across her pretty face. "Yes, Harvey has seen to all my needs," she answered out of irritation. "As well as dealing wiz your little crazy and caring for zee medical needs of zee pack." There was no question that Clarise was more dominant than Harvey.

It was one thing for Analise to talk to him that way. It was another entirely for Rhys to hear it from a true stock werewolf. His eyes were molten and slammed into her light blues with seething anger. Clarise held out as long as she could, but eventually broke the eye contact with a huff and a flip of her blonde hair.

That's right, Rhys retorted in his own mind.

"I suppose you are here to order us to care for your little crazy, zen?" She remarked through a sigh. Harvey cast her a pleading look to stop, but Rhys beat him to the comment.

"Actually, I'm here to apologize to Harv for that shiner," He answered confidently before turning his glance at Harvey. "And to invite you both to dinner sometime. Sure would like to get to know this little French poodle of yours," he added, much to Clarise's irritation.

Harvey visibly relaxed. "Don't worry about it," he answered casually. "I let you down. Figure I deserved a lot worse... "

"Deserved a lot worse!" Let out Clarise in dismay. This was followed by a huff and a stream of unintelligible French cursing.

Rhys largely dismissed her, more concerned about his brother. "You were gonna kill her," he commented, still a bit stunned. "I just sort of reacted but I shoulda thought about it first."

Harvey shrugged. "I didn't know what to do, Rhys," he commented, leaning back into his chair. "I've never even heard of a turn going that badly before, let alone experienced it." Harvey gazed absently at Clarise, who was fuming with irritation for Rhys. "The girl's tough though, I'll give her that," he added in a distant voice. "Every bone in her body must have snapped at least a dozen times but she still refused to let the wolf take over."

Rhys frowned slightly. "Yeah, she's pretty stubborn," he commented in the same absent tone Harvey had donned. "Look, Harv, I need her medical records. Shepherd seems to think that you'll have written stuff in there that gives it up that she's a were now."

Harvey offered Rhys a critical frown. "I'm not an idiot, Rhys," he replied dryly. "It's as squeaky clean as a babe in a bath. No one's gonna find anything in there."

"All the same," Rhys returned, "I'd rather be safe than sorry. That woman's already been surprisingly accurate with her were-knowledge and if what she's saying about those two FBI agents I've got in my office down town is true, we can't take any risks." Rhys considered his brother for a moment. "Maybe you or Clarise could bring them to her," he volunteered."

Clarise scoffed. "Why in zee world would I want to socialize wiz zat woman? She is a hunter, no?"

"She's one of us now," Rhys answered confidently. "Whether or not any of us, Analise included, likes it, she's one of us. I'm sure this ain't as fancy as you're used to, Clarise, but everyone here is safe from hunters because we all stick together and look out for each other." Rhys consciously stepped off of his pedastool. "Besides," he added with a shrug, "You two seem to have a lot in common."

Harvey sighed slightly. "I'll bring her the files later," he relented.

"Good," Rhys said with a half smile and a nod. "Now. Where am I taking you two for dinner tonight?"

It was several hours later that Rhys found himself in the hospital again. Isa had done as he had asked and saw to it that Agent Shepherd was moved to a recovery ward in Riverton Medical and Harvey had delivered the files as promised. Rhys was grateful for things to work out for a change. He had a mountain of paperwork waiting for him at the precinct and it wasn't until he had lost track of time that he realized he was about to be late for the dinner date with Harvey and Clarise.

So, he returned to the hospital and strolled down to Harvey's secretary only to learn that Harvey was attending Shepherd while the other two agents talked to her. A chill ran down Rhys's spine. He had been so focused in his own work that he forgot to keep an eye on Agent Peters.

Rhys carefully paced his steps as he made it to the recovery ward. He didn't want anyone to know that his natural urge was to run in so he counted his steps very carefully. The beauty of being a werewolf, however, was that Rhys's hearing was phenomenal. He could hear the conversation between the FBI agents from well down the hall.

"Thanks," Analise commented to Harvey as he finished taking her blood pressure.

Agent Peters tightened his eyes. "What did you say your name was again, doctor?"

"Harvey Forrester," he replied tersely. "Look, she really needs to rest and I'm not-"

"As in Captain Forrester's brother?" Peters continued smoothly.

Analise rolled her eyes. "Yeah, Frank, it's a small town. You are surprised by this, why? The whole place is inbred."

Rhys could almost hear Harvey growl in irritation at Analise.

"Doctor, if you would excuse us..." Agent Peters suggested in his strange, fluid tone.

"It's fine, Dr. Forrester," Analise added. "I'm feeling a lot better. If you see Captain Forrester, could you let him know that I'm still waiting on those case files?" Rhys smirked. She was certainly feeling back to normal if the all-work-and-no-play Analise was back.

Harvey frowned, sighed heavily, and left the room. As he made it down the hall, his expression changed from professional irritation to worry. Rhys had expected as much. Harvey trotted over and gestured for Rhys to sit with him on a bench in the hospital hallway. Rhys gestured for Harvey to be quiet and his brother nodded, joining him in the eaves dropping of the Agents' conversation.

"What do you want, Frank," Analise let out in a tired and irritated sigh.

"I merely find it interesting that Captain Forrester has taken up such an interest in your well being that he would request his brother to do a nurse's job in monitoring you," Peters replied smoothly.

Analise rolled her eyes again. "A Federal Agent was assault in his town. I don't think it's peculiar at all. He's terrified that we'll press charges or something. Anyway, I've got this situation under control. You still haven't told me why you are here."

"Under control?" Let out Agent Carter in a concerned voice. Unlike Peters, Carter seemed to be a genuinely nice guy. "Analise, you said it yourself: you were assaulted! Are you ok?"

"Yeah, I'm fine. A couple bruises is all," she replied dismissively.

Peters wasn't buying it. "An a concussion that rendered you unconscious for almost a week," he added. "At least, according to the medical records..." It didn't take a genius to see that he didn't believe what he read and Rhys was suddenly curious about what Analise had changed there.

Analise offered Frank an irritated glare. "As is documented in my own report, we were attacked by the cultists and I pursued them. I was ambushed and during the struggle I was rendered unconscious. Captain Forrester's report clearly states that his team approached the scene and was driven to use lethal force in subduing the targets. I previously had estimated 5-6 cultists based off activity levels, which is the number of targets that were killed in the conflict, which means that this cell has been neutralized and it brings me to my original question of why you are here?"

"It's standard procedure to dispatch personnel when an agent has been injured in the line of duty," Carter answered calmly. "But no one is questioning the thoroughness of your work, Analise. And Captain Forrester has been very accommodating in getting us your notes too."

"Yes, he has been very accommodating," Peters commented dryly. "Tell me, Agent Shepherd, what is your relationship with Captain Forrester?"

Both Rhys and Harvey went wide-eyed at the question. Analise, on the other hand, didn't miss a beat. "He's my boyfriend," she offered both casually and dismissively, as if it were nothing at all. "You'll have to excuse me for not filing the appropriate conflict of interest forms while I was in a coma, but even still, I fail to see what relevance that has on this investigation."

Carter looked a bit stunned. "You... you are... I shouldn't ask. I'm very happy for you, Analise," he told her kindly. Rhys decided then that he liked Agent Carter. He seemed to care about Analise.

"Actually, you should ask," Peters continued smoothly. "Because it strictly against Bureau policy to fraternize with local law enforcement."

Analise wondered if her eyes would continue to roll like this indefinitely. "You are more than welcome to take it up with our supervisor, Frank," she told him dryly. "I'm sure he'll get a kick out of that sort of complaint anyway. Besides, when I called him to request a leave of absence, he basically mandated it anyway. Not really sure what else you'd be hoping to accomplish there, but knock yourself out."

Peter's eyed her critically. "Unfortunately, Analise, your relationship with Captain Forrester is of interest in this investigation."

"And why's that," she commented in irritation.

"Because it is highly suspicious that you would become romantically involved with him."

"Oh I know," Analise returned in full sarcasm. "I mean, how could a woman be attracted to a soft spoken gentleman cowboy with beautiful blue eyes and ripply muscles. What in the world was I thinking? And for him to be attracted to me? Well, something is clearly wrong with this situation..." Harvey smirked and jabbed Rhys in the side with his elbow.

"Your records were unclear: does Captain Forrester have any involvement with the cult?" Any lightheartedness the brothers had been feeling evaporated with Agent Peters' forward and blunt question.

"Jesus Christ, Frank," Analise reprimanded sharply. "Do you honestly think I'm that big of an idiot? Of course he doesn't; that's absurd. No one in this town does; I was very thorough in that. The kidnappers were drifters and nothing more. In fact, a lot of locals commented on the number of strangers lately and if anything, these little river towns are probably going to shut themselves off to the outside world after this incident."

Peters didn't believe her, but he didn't argue. "I will bring you the conflict of interest form. Of course, I will be inquiring with Director Forbes about the status of this investigation. It has been assigned to me in your interim."

"Congratulations," she offered dryly.

"That wound on your neck...?" He added as he and Carter were preparing to leave. Rhys's anxiety level had swelled so high that he was already on his feet heading toward her room.

"Yeah, I got in a bar fight," Analise answered smoothly. "I'm sure you already talked to my lawyer about it. One of the assholes bit me. I think it's infected too... Dr. Forrester has been concerned, from what I've been told, because they tried a round of antibiotics when they found it after the assault but obviously I was allergic, which they didn't know, and it screwed up my blood work. All of this is in the medical records you certainly read, Frank. Trust me, if it was a cultist who bit me, I'd have reported it right away."

Rhys entered the room in time to watch Agent Peters offer Analise a condescending smile. "That's good to hear," he answered smoothly. "Ah. Your significant other."

Rhys offered Peters a sour look. "You told 'em then?" He nodded to Analise as if to silently will to her that he had heard the whole thing. "Gentlemen," he offered them both with a lift of his hat and a polite nod. "If it's alright with you, I'd like to have a word with Analise."

"Of course," Carter said in understanding. "We were just leaving, right Frank?"

Agent Peters looked like he was on the verge of sneering.

"I, uh, I didn't know what the right form number was," Rhys told her, pretending to be a bit sheepish. "Looks like there are a lot of forms for conflict of interest. Maybe one of your friends here could grab it for you?"

"How fortuitous," Agent Peters said, the condescention in his tone seeming to have grown. "I have a copy right here. I've taken the liberty of filling out your respective names. Unfortunately, I was unable to locate an original birth certificate for you, Captain, so I was unable to apply your date of birth."

"You coulda just asked," Rhys stated firmly. "Court house burnt down several years back. We only got copies of things. Did you have any particular reason to be looking into our records, Agent Peters?"

"Forgive me, I thought it was a matter of public record," he replied smoothly. He was right, of course. "And I didn't want to trust a copy. Pity, really. So all of the city records were lost in this fire?"

Analise let out a long and impatient sigh. "Yeah, as Jim just said, Frank and Jim were just leaving. Thanks, Frank, but I will fill out the form from here. Let me know when you've talked with Forbes. My understanding is that I am the lead on this investigation and I am closing it. Take it up with Forbes if you want that changed."

Agent Peters offered a smirking nod and Agent Carter ushered him out of the room. From down the hall, both Analise and Rhys could hear Carter lecturing Peters on being rude. Analise let out a sigh of relief as the pair made their way out of the hospital. Only after this exasperation did she turn her tired eyes to Rhys.

"You heard all of that, I gather?" She inquired smoothly.

"One of the perks of our kind, I suppose," He acknowledged while taking a seat along the side of her bed. "How are you feeling?"

"Stop asking," she remarked. "I'm fine. Look... about the whole... well..." She paused to dismiss her own awkwardness. "I think I need to stick around for a while until I get a handle on what's happening to me," she finally admitted. "Between that and all of your attention, I figured a relationship was the best way to call off Frank's curiosity. I'm more than happy to explain all of this to your girlfriend and I swear I'll even be nice when I do it."

Rhys smirked at her. "No need to worry. I don't have one," he answered before becoming slightly playful. "Though, it's real sweet that you find me attractive, Analise. You aren't too bad yourself."

Analise snorted and blushed slightly. "Oh get over it. You know you're pretty. Look, it's a weird situation, but it's all I could come up with to keep Peters at bay. It shouldn't be that bad. I'll play nice if you do. With any luck, Peters will buy it and go back home."

"I don't know, Analise. What exactly does a pretend boyfriend do? Besides, half the time I'm wanting to punch you in the face. Certainly isn't something I'd do if you were my girl." Rhys was obviously uncomfortable with this entire topic.

"Well, it's good that you don't punch me in the face Rhys," she added, obviously finding his behavior to be strange. "That's called assault and I'm definitely not into that... Honestly, just keep up the interest in my well being. You don't have to do anything affectionate or anything. I think it would just make Peters more suspicious if you did. I'm not really the affectionate type, you may have heard."

Rhys cocked an eyebrow at her. "And what is your type?"

Analise cast him a bored expression. "Soft spoken gentleman cowboy with pretty eyes and ripply muscles," she answered through a smirk. "You?"

Rhys was smirking too. "Sweet and quiet overweight housewife type. Looks like it's not meant to be."

Analise actually laughed at the comment. "Alright, alright. What's your pretend date of birth so I can fill this thing out."

Rhys was having trouble sleeping. His dreams seemed to be a repeat of Agent Peters shooting him in the gut and forcing him to watch as the Agents systematically slaughtered his pack. In the end, it kept returning to Aru demanding that he be let out and Rhys suddenly was thrust awake as he felt himself involuntarily shift. He jerked in his bed, shoving at the blankets and propping himself half up on his elbow. It was then that he noticed a pair of bright green eyes watching him.

Analise's wolf sat at the edge of the bed, offering him a wolfish grin while her spoon shaped tongue hung out and panted slightly. "Aruuu" she let out in a happy yelp.

Rhys was a bit alarmed. Not only had Analise shifted (probably without her consent) but her wolf was eliciting an involuntary shift out of him. Rhys swallowed hard as he fought Aru back down using every compromise and promise in the book. "... Analise what are you doing?" He let out in a tired sigh as he pushed the blankets back and swung his feet over the edge of the bed. It had been a long and stressful day, and even the pleasant dinner he had with Harvey and Clarise wasn't taking the edge off of his worry. That Analise in wolf form was sitting in his dark room staring at him didn't make him worry any less.

Of course, this wasn't Analise, per say. This was her wolf and Rhys didn't actually expect the animal to understand him. The dog moved to stand in between his legs, nudging his abs gently with her snout before looking up again at him with an expectant doggy smile. This wolf was far more docile and domesticated than any he knew, probably owing to Analise not being a true werewolf but a turn.

Rhys was tired but offered the creature an amused smile. He pushed his hands over her head, rubbing behind her ears and petting her precisely how he would any friendly dog. "You silly dog," he told her in a kind voice. "She's not going to be happy that you did this. You should head back before she figures it out."

To his surprise, the wolf jumped up, resting her paws on his legs, and smothered his face in dog licks.

Analise's wolf, though she clearly thought otherwise, was not a tiny little lap dog. The weight of her landing on him and the force of her snout in his face was enough to push Rhys backward, even with his attempt to resist it. Still, as unexpected as it was, Rhys found himself chuckling in response, still petting the side of her head as he tried to push her away.

"Aruuuu," she let out again. This dog was just as persistent as Analise any day of the week. It was no wonder that they were constantly butting heads.

"Ok, ok, I'll let him out," he told her through his own chuckles.

The wolf jumped down and did an excited swirl, like a dog happily anticipating her owner to throw her favorite ball. She yelped and yipped happily as she waited for him to give her what she had come for. "Just one thing," he told her as he pulled his tee shirt off. "What's your name? What I should I call you, girl?"

"Rheaaaa," the dog yelped at him, clearly excited that they were talking and very happy to introduce herself.

"Rhea, huh? That's a very nice name. Did Analise give that to you?"

The dog yelped happily in the affirmative. Interesting, Rhys thought as he pulled off his shorts. Apparently Analise had at least taken that much of his advice. It was also interesting to him that Rhea seemed to be understanding him pretty well. It usually took wolves years to figure out human speech well enough to carry on a conversation of this level. It was impressive, actually, that Rhea was such an effective communicator. "Well, it's a pleasure to meet you Rhea. I'll have Aru to you in just a second. Can you show me where you got in at?" It was another piece of the puzzle.

Rhea trotted over to the open window and yelped at it. Rhys frowned slightly at this. He was on the second floor and there was no fire escape for Rhea to climb. He thought about asking her how she managed this, but Aru was starting to claw at him from inside. This would be a discussion for another time, he figured. Rhys cast Rhea a pleased grin and made his way over to the door. "We're probably going to have leave this way," he told her. "Aru isn't a great jumper. There are doggie doors like this all over the den; you can use these instead of the window if you want in the future."

Rhea cocked her head curiously at the doggy door and trotted forward to examine it. She sniffed at it and resumed her wolf grin. "Aru!" she yelped happily, obviously picking up his scent. Next she pawed at it and then jumped backward as the flap swung slightly. Her ears folded backward but then pushed forward again as she continued her exploration of the apparently interesting contraption. Rhys had to chuckle at her. Rhea was easy going and constantly happy. He instantly liked her and figured everyone else would too.

"I might have to have you meet the pack before Analise does," he said happily, crouching down to rest one arm over her back, scratching behind her ear, as he lifted the flap up for her to see past it. "See? Just the hallway over there. These are all over the den. You think you could come in and out this way?"

Rhea barked again in the affirmative and then spun happily, licking Rhys's face a few times and then again insisting for Aru.

"Ok, ok, here you go," he let up in false retreat. In an instant, Rhys shifted and in his place stood a large grey wolf. Rhea barked and yelped happily, doing her spinning happy dance as soon as he was there.

"Aru!" she announced happily. "Come! We run!"

"Yeah!" Aru let out just as happily as she was. What almost no one knew was that Rhys hardly ever let Aru out, particularly for something as pointless as running around. For the most of their shared life, Aru remained sadly caged away, silently sighing because he had no one to play with. Once Rhea started to assert herself, though, he demanded that Rhys let them play.

Rhea barked and then pushed through the doggy door, quickly followed by Aru. Given that Rhys had been in the den, no one questioned a pair of wolves trotting together through the hallways of the den. In fact, several people smiled at them and held the doors open as they made their way to the exit. Each time, Rhea let out a grateful and happy yelp, eliciting smiles and chuckles for those who assisted them. As Rhys had predicted, Rhea was instantly likeable. While no one recognized Rhea, more than a few people recognized Aru and the sight of their alpha running around frivolously went a long way toward calming high strung emotions in the pack.

Within a few moments, the pair made their way outside and were trotting to a nearby glade. "Aru we run!" Rhea proposed happily as she trotted in a circle around Aru.

"Yeah!" He answered again, nipping playfully at her tail as she passed by.

"Ready... go!" She shouted, first lowering her front half and wiggling her haunch in anticipation, and then breaking into the fastest sprint Aru had ever witnessed. Her ears folded back and she dashed like the wind.

"Wait for me!" Aru shouted after her, but he was never able to close the gap that had built. Rhea was considerably faster than he was and even after she made it to their randomly determined finish line, she wasn't even winded. Aru, on the other hand, was panting heavily. "You fast," he told her. "Wrestle?"

"Yeah!" Rhea answered happily, jumping up in the air with excitement.

Aru let out a happy yelp of his own and promptly launched himself at Rhea. The wolf dodged him fairly easily and then rolled slightly to pounce on him in return. Aru allowed her to land and then shifted his weight so that Rhea would lose her footing. The tactic worked and in an instant, Aru had tackled her to the ground, playfully biting at her ear while she attempted to gnaw at his jowls.

This pattern of play continued for hours. They would run long distances and then they would wrestle, followed by more running and more wrestling. The results were always the same: Rhea always won the races and Aru always won the wrestling, though Rhea was getting better at dodging him. Both Rhea and Aru determined, but the end of it all, that they were evenly matched and, interestingly, they decided to forgo the dominance challenges entirely, agreeing that they should cooperate as equals.

Only a human would have made it more complicated than that. The wolves had tested each other and determined that they were both strong and had complimentary strengths. That was all they needed to know to make this determination. Aru and Rhea were instant best friends for life and nothing anyone could say or do would change that.

Sometime after a countless number of races and wrestling matches, Aru looked up at the sky and then laid down, looking sadly on as Rhea continued to pounce around in a field, chasing after a rabbit. Rhea saw him and trotted up, with her spoon tongue hanging happily between her wolf grin. "Aru sad," she commented. "Why sad?"

"Want stay with Rhea," he replied in a whine. "Can't. Human say go back now."

Rhea growled slightly in disappointment. "No. Aru and Rhea stay!" She proposed happily. "Run! Wrestle! Eat food!"

Aru turned his head away in a sad sigh. "No. Aru want stay with Rhea but male human want female human now. Human say we play later. Go back now."

Rhea laid down in front of him and nudged his head with her muzzle. "Human mean," she said in a huff. "Rhea want stay with Aru." Rhea took on an inquisitive look suddenly. "Male human make female human give us play?" She asked hopefully.

Aru yelped in the affirmative, suddenly lifting his spirits. "Yes! Tomorrow night we play again! Male human make promise!"

"OK!" Rhea let out happily. She jumped to her feet and did her happy tail chaise dance. "Tomorrow we play again! Yeah!"

Aru was leased at this compromise and wagged his tail happily, jumping up to lick at her face. "We go to den now?"

"Ok!" Rhea agreed, already turning to trot in the correct direction.

When Analise opened her eyes later, she instantly realized that she was not where she thought she should have been. She was laying in Rhys's bed, curled up against him and in his arms while his hand gently caressed the small of her back, rather than in her hospital bed where she had fallen asleep. Analise slowly looked up to Rhys, who was staring contemplatively at the ceiling. Analise was confused, but not as alarmed as she thought she should have been. "... you know... if I keep waking up in your bed like this, it's not going to be too hard to convince Peters about this dating business we're falsifying."

Rhys's lips curled into an amused smirk. "I think you shifted in your sleep," he told her gently. "Rhea and Aru had a lot of fun chasing rabbits, from what I gather," he added. "There was some reluctance to return."

Analise's good humored expression melted slightly. "... what? She told you her name? And she was chasing rabbits?... please tell me I didn't eat one... "

Rhys let out a humored chuckle. "Yeah, she told me and no, no rabbits were harmed in the making of their play time."

"Precisely what else did play time entail?" She inquired without missing a beat.

Rhys turned his head, his deep blue eyes looking into hers. "Aru won't do that without my permission," he told her firmly, albeit in a friendly tone, "and I won't give him that permission without first getting yours," he finished, feeling her tension melt in his arms.

"Ok," she answered in relief. Analise obviously had no control over Rhea and knowing that Rhys could reel in Aru gave her a great deal of comfort. "Well, I'm glad they had a good time then," she added.

"I promised Aru that they could play again tomorrow," he told her hesitantly. "Rhea wasn't going to relinquish control at all and for a second there I thought she'd convince Aru not to shift back. She ended up proposing that we let them play together in the evenings as some sort of compromise. Aru wouldn't let go until I promised to make that happen... "

Analise gave him another alarmed look as she propped herself up to glare at him with worry. "... can... they can do that?" Panic was evident in her tone.

Rhys nodded a bit. "Like I said, you gotta work things out between the two of you. Not just your body anymore; sort of like being pregnant, I guess," he realized that while he didn't know what maternity was like, he did understand the idea of sharing a body with someone else. In that concept, he figured he was more knowledgeable than the average male. "I... I didn't really have a chance to ask you first but I figured it would get ugly for us both if I didn't. Rhea's pretty stubborn. Like someone else I know."

Analise sunk back down and let out a dejected sigh. "I should probably move near you until I can get her under control. I'm really sorry about this," she offered through a pathetic sigh. "I have no idea who saw her trotting through the hospital to get... where ever I am...?"

"You're in the den; in my apartment. I was worried about the same thing, though," he told her. "I'm guessing Rhea came straight here too so there was no illusion about what was going on."

Analise closed her eyes to steady her patience with... herself. "I had no idea," she offered, almost apologetically. "I remember falling asleep and I woke up here. Is... that's not common is it?"

Rhys shook his head. "All depends on how dominant the pair is. You're both pretty dominant, which means you are suppressing Rhea when you are "awake" and she suppresses you when it's her turn. Your case is probably the most extreme I've seen, but it's not new to our kind."

Analise was watching him closely, studying his expressions. A gentle silence fell between them before she finally spoke again. "I've got to ask you a favor," she offered finally.

This piqued Rhys's interest and he turned to offer her a curious look.

"I need to go back to Boston. I need... I'm guessing that I need to move out here for a while and I need to make a more stable arrangement about my cat and my mail and stuff." She continued looking at him, expecting him to connect the dots. When he didn't, she concluded, "Could you go with me? I don't trust myself at all with this right now and I need someone who can keep little miss Rhea from running wild down the streets of Boston."

Rhys raised both eyebrows, surprised by the proposition. "... I've actually never left Riverton before," he admitted painfully. "I'm happy to go, Analise, but... I don't know how much help I'll be if I'm that far out of my element..."

Analise grinned in a way that reminded him very much of the easy going Rhea grin. "Oh don't worry," she assured him. "I'll take care of Rhys as far as city life goes. I just need a babysitter for when I fall asleep," she answered finally, still offering him a friendly grin.

It was Rhys's turn to look painfully unsure of himself as he offered her a confused frown. "Look," she continued through a sigh. "We'd only be gone a few days. I know you've got this "Rhys is in charge" thing going on, but it isn't like this place will fall apart in just a few days? And if something does happen, can't that brother of yours handle it? Or what's her name, that french girl I hate. What's her name?"

"Clarise," he told her, still not liking where this idea was going.

"Yeah, Clarise. As much as I dislike her, she has her shit together," Analise volunteered in what was probably the most reasonable defense anyone had ever offered on behalf of Clarise. "That, and, I get the idea that she's shacking up with your brother so do you honestly think she'd let anything happen around here?" Analise considered what she was saying for a moment. "Actually, for that matter, who's that old- Isa! Isa's like your own guru or something. Yeah... here's what you do:" she started as if Analise had any say in the matter. The woman wouldn't have known that up until that moment, Isa was the only person to ever offer Rhys any sort of advice on pack management matters. "Tell your brother that he and his girlfriend are in charge while you're gone and if anything comes up that they can't figure out, they should go ask Isa," she told him confidently. "Your brother will be all happy that you trust him, Clarise will be the one who probably takes care of anything but that way she doesn't feel like she's stepping out of line or anything, and Isa won't feel kicked to the curb. Everyone wins and I get my escort for the week, plus, you get to take what I have determined is a much needed vacation on my dime."

Rhys couldn't argue. That was pretty sound logic. Analise was going to be better at pack dynamics than she realized. As for the part where she paid for his trip, however, Rhys could only glower at her sourly.

Analise rolled her eyes. "Consider it payment for pretending to be my boyfriend and baby sitting my pet wolf while I'm not around," she offered with a snort as she pushed herself out of the bed and tugged the top blanket up and around her. "Paying for your expenses is the least I can do."

Rhys finally determined what it was he didn't like about this arrangement and sat up to offer Analise a cross expression. "No." he answered solidly.

Analise turned to offer him a confused look. She hadn't been expecting that sort of response.

"No to all of it. I ain't gonna pretend to be your boyfriend. Either I am or I am not. Not where feelings like those are involved. Now I get it; you're scared out of your mind. You have been for the last thirty or so years, always thinking the big bad wolf was gonna grab you next, watching what the loss of your sister did to your family. Now you're scared that your own people ain't gonna understand what just happened to you; that you're a target now."

"I get that, Analise, because I'm scared too. Every night I go to bed wondering if I'm ever gonna wake up again or if this is my last day. I'm afraid because I've got a pretty big family to look after and it only takes one screw up for your people to be on us in an instant. I'm terrified that I'm gonna mess all this up and watch my family be slaughtered for it. And I am damn sick of hiding in fear and constantly playing pretend with every aspect of my life just so I can keep on living in fear so I sure as hell am not gonna do it with my love life too." Rhys nearly barked at her, the words left him so firmly. While Harvey may have guessed that Rhys felt this overwhelmed, he had never before articulated. Analise was the first person that Rhys even remotely felt could understand this stress that he wore every day.

Analise was a bit daunted by the lecture that Rhys delivered and she slowly sat back down on the edge of the bed, watching him with a mixture of sympathy, guilt, and deep understanding. "I... I'm sorry, Rhys," she told him honestly. "I didn't mean... I mean... "

"Look, I said I get it," he told her dismissively enough. "Analise, none of this is in our hands. Never was. You and I are afraid of the same thing from two different sides of the same coin and to be perfectly honest, I'm happy to have met you because... well, hell, I ain't afraid to go to sleep because I figure you got my back if something goes wrong. Now you think of that what you will, but I never thought I'd live long enough for that sort of relief and I sure as hell ain't gonna trivialize it by pretending to be your boyfriend just to throw a few or your people off my scent."

Analise was still and silent, her eyes drifting aimlessly forward as she listened to everything Rhys was telling her. "I'm a mess, Rhys," she finally told him. "Yeah, I've got your back," she shrugged slightly, "and I get the feeling that you're looking out for me, so, I mean, that's appreciated, but I'm still a mess. You're right; I am afraid. I have been ever since Laura went missing. Every time another little girl gets nabbed, I get scared for her. Now I have another thing that scares me: your pack. Now I get to be worried about what happens when my people show up and hurt all of those innocent people. Now I have to wonder how many innocent lives I've destroyed out of my own fear, and that's not a pleasant thought, I assure you. "

She turned to look at Rhys, curious about how he was absorbing all of this information. "It all traces back to one point. There is one thing responsible for all of this fear," she said definitively. Rhys knew full well what she was implying and his eyes widened slightly. It was suicide to take on the council. Only a turn as new as Analise would be ignorant enough to venture otherwise. Perhaps this was a trait of being a High Alpha? Isa had mentioned something along these lines, of their extreme ways of thinking. Still, her green eyes pierced into his with an intensity he had never before experienced. Rhys knew what she was going to do and he knew she wouldn't be doing it alone.

"Having each other's backs isn't good enough," she told him finally. "You say you aren't going to short change your love life? Then why would you settle for anything other than freedom. You want to be my boyfriend? I kind of like the sound of that; of being able to finally let down my guard enough to let someone in." The intensity of her gaze hadn't stopped. "So, are you going to help me take down this Council of yours or not?"

THE END